THE LIAR'S CORNER
The Saga Continues

*Another two and a half years
of laughter from the*
Nebraska Farmer's
Liar's Corner

Roger Welsch

Fall 1988–Winter 1991

Other books by Roger Welsch include
It's Not the End of the Earth But You Can See It From Here
Touching the Fire: Buffalo Dancers, the Sky Bundle,
   and Other Tales
Catfish at the Pump
Shingling the Fog
Mister, You Got Yourself a Horse
You Know You're a Nebraskan When . . . (with Paul Fell)
Treasury of Nebraska Pioneer Folklore
The Liar's Corner

ISBN 0-934904-32-4

J & L Lee Co. • P.O. Box 5575 • Lincoln, NE 68505

For Eric

Roger Welsch has dedicated 35 years of his life to the examination of American folk humor, not only—he points out—because humor is important to an understanding of America and especially its frontier, but because "No one enjoys those stories and jokes more than I do!" When Welsch began writing The Liar's Corner column for the *Nebraska Farmer* magazine in 1985, he lived in Lincoln, Nebraska, and taught at the University of Nebraska. Since then he has, as he says, "taken my own advice and moved to the rural countryside, where the very best of American humor is still alive and laughing."

Open these pages and you will be laughing too. Welcome again to the Liar's Corner and Roger Welsch's storytelling friends . . .

A MODEST INTRODUCTION

Right off, let's get this straight: I don't tell lies. My task is to pass along what I hear, and that's what I do. I am told now and then that some of the stories I print in my *Nebraska Farmer* column, The Liar's Corner, may not be altogether factual. Well, the names of the folks who have sent me these stories are right here for everyone to see, so pass along your complaints to them.

Me? There's a reason why everyone in Dannebrog calls me "Honest Rog." (Well, *almost* everyone.)

If you want a brief history of how the Liar's Corner came to be resurrected in the *Nebraska Farmer* magazine seven years ago, you'll find it all in the introduction to the first volume of this set, *The Liar's Corner,* published in 1988 by Plains Heritage, Dannebrog, Nebraska. Since that book was published, things have gone pretty much the same for the Liar's Corner. I would have guessed that *Nebraska Farmer* readers would have tired of the whole idea a long time ago, but the stories continue to roll in, almost every day, and the folks I encounter in my travels continue to tell me that the first thing they turn to when they get their *Nebraska Farmer* is the Liar's Corner.

I also would have guessed that I would have gotten tired of this after seven years, but I am as enthusiastic as ever. As far as I can tell, the traditionally rich sense of humor that characterized our Plains frontier and which continued to prosper on the Plains rural countryside is, if anything, growing even more lively. Sure, I get a lot of the same old stories I have been getting for seven years— many of them already published in earlier columns—but it is the rare month that goes by without a couple of new knee-slappers coming my way, stories I immediately haul on up to town to try on my friends Harriett, Dee, Gaylord, Chancey, Lyle, Eric, Dan, Bondo . . . the whole zany crowd.

I hope you find your name and story in these pages, but if you don't, there is a solution to your disappointment: send me a story right away and you'll probably be in the next volume. (As I suggest in almost every issue of the *Nebraska Farmer,* you can send your stories to me at Ol' Rog, Primrose Farm, Dannebrog, Nebraska 68831, and Lyle the Mailman will see to it that it gets to me.)

I owe a lot of people gratitude for what you find here. Of course, first of all I thank all of you who took the time and trouble to send me jokes, stories, anecdotes, puzzles, wisecracks, and tall tales. I must also express my gratitude to Dave Howe, editor of the *Nebraska Farmer*, and Bob Bishop, his predecessor, for taking the risks of including a humor column in a serious economic and professional agriculture magazine, often during difficult times; I hope I have deserved your confidence. Diane Reverand and Villard Books kindly gave me permission to publish this book outside of the provisions of my contract with them, a kindness which I very much appreciate.

I write the same thing in every book I write and in every book I mean it more sincerely: I owe eternal gratitude to my wife Lovely Linda for putting up with my growly moods when I am writing, for carefully reading manuscripts and proofs (and systematically refusing to take credit for her contributions), for protecting me from kind but uninvited visitors, for telling me when I have dumb ideas (like the time I bought four ancient Allis Chalmers WC tractors in one day) and then not killing me when I ignore her (like the time I bought four ancient Allis Chalmers WC tractors in one day), and for putting aside her own considerable talents to let me realize my modest ones. I wish I had her wit, but I'll settle for her companionship.

And that, as always, is the truth. As for what follows, well, as I said when I started off this modest introduction, I am only repeating what you and your friends sent to me at the Liar's Corner . . .

HOT AND DRY

1

Summer was a good time for stories, because they came rolling in at a good pace!

Sorry Charlie is one of Dannebrog's least distinguished citizens. He thinks he's had a rough day when he has to deal the cards twice in one morning. Anyway, Harriett's Danish Cafe recently had a special: two pancakes at the regular price, two more for one cent. Sorry Charlie stumbled in and told Harriett that all he wanted was the third and fourth pancakes, because he wasn't hungry enough for the first two.

Dee Steffenhagen was the waitress at the time and I forget exactly what she said, but when she got done, Sorry Charlie moved along about as briskly as he did the last time someone said, "Your turn to buy, Charlie!"

One of the most underestimated senses of humor in Nebraska is that of Charlie Thone, former governor of Nebraska and quite a different person from Sorry Charlie. I have had the marvelous opportunity of spending many hours, sitting beside Charlie Thone at head tables at various banquets, and I have always relished those occasions for the stories that Charlie can tell. (And before you think that this is some sort of partisan politicking, I would like to note that I am a lifelong, unregenerate Democrat.)

Perhaps one of my favorites is the one Charlie tells about his mother, when she sent him off into the world with good advice. "They can fool you once," she said, "And they can fool you twice. But don't let them fool you a second time."

Senator Jerry Warner's line recently has been, when someone asks him what he's raising on his farm, "Debt."

Gary Wulf, and ace announcer at KZ100 in Central City, says that they recently had a "dry" humor contest at the station to commemorate the tough summer. Curiously, two of the stories Gary sent as winners were two that I awarded as winners in this column! I guess that speaks to the popularity of Gary and KZ100. Gary's favorite, and mine, is the one about the new law they had to pass—no more water skiing on the Platte River. Seems it was kicking up too much dust.

Gene Kyhn of Boelus jumped in on a conversation about how spotty the rain has been by saying that he was hilling corn this summer and at one end of the row he could hardly see for the dust. And he got stuck in the mud at the other end.

Frankly, I think Harlan Kroeger came up with the topper when he said that he had seen what the drouth situation was like in North Dakota and he is planning to truck some of his cows up there just to show them how lucky they are!

NO COMPETITION

2

I never know what to think when I encounter a clutch of story-tellers all from one locality. Should I draw what seems the natural conclusion? That the place is packed with liars? Well, that's what happened when I was in Tecumseh last May for the centennial rededication of the Johnson County Courthouse.

First, Howard Wilkinson of the County Board told me about his uncle who was once out in a Johnson County field, stealing watermelons. Seems the farmer heard the dogs barking and went out to fire a couple of loads of buckshot across the top of the field.

Asked later if he was afraid, Howard's uncle replied, "No, I wasn't. But I passed up two guys who were."

Then Don Seeba of the Johnson County Chamber of Commerce topped things off, and it always unsettles me when I hear someone from a Chamber of Commerce who is so obviously an accomplished liar. Don told the gathered dignitaries that it was once so bitterly cold that he had to go out to the creek to cut some wood to keep the house warm.

Don says that he was chopping so fast that his ax got hot and he had to go back to the house to get another one so he could let one ax cool as he chopped with the other. But even that didn't solve the hot ax problem, so he chopped a hole in the ice of the creek so he could cool the hot ax heads in the water.

But then the hot choppers heated up the creek so bad that it wouldn't cool the axes any more, so he just had to quit for the day.

"But that was okay," Don added. "My chips had started to come down about then and I couldn't see to chop anyway."

Congressman Doug Bereuter was next on the program and I

think he was going to tell us how much the Republican Administration had done for farmers this past year but he was so outclassed he just mumbled something about being glad to be there and sat down.

I think he is hoping that Don Seeba and Howard Wilkinson don't run for Congress the next election.

NO LIE, CAVETT ATTENDED

3

November 5, 1988

Last week it was time for the 37th Annual Awards Banquet of the National Liars Hall of Fame in Dannebrog, Nebraska. It was, as always, a gala event, attended by a white-tie crowd that overflowed the Grand Salon at the Hall of Fame.

The meal consisted of baloney and ham, a Hall of Fame specialty, and celebrity comedians in attendance were Letterman, Hope, Rivers, and Cosby. (Fred Letterman, Loretta Hope, Frank Rivers, and Chuckie Crosby from over by Farwell.) A novelty gift from the Liar's Hall of Fame was a seed catalog for the spring of 1989 at each diner's plate.

Inducted into the National Liars Hall of Fame and joining the giants of prevarication whose names are already engraved on the faux gold plaques was Johnny Carson, honored because his contributions to the art of Tall Tale. The frequent inclusion in Johnny's monologue of his "How cold was it?" "How windy was it?" "How dumb was he?" stories is profoundly reminiscent of his Plains heritage and reminds the world of the importance of well-crafted exaggeration.

A public service award went to Dick Cavett, who actually was in attendance, for his work with his syndicated radio program, "The Comedy Show," which has made a major contribution to American humor by having me on it.

The annual Pinocchio Award went to Russell Hoy, columnist for the *Ohio Farmer,* who told one about the Great Drouth of '88. He had me fooled for a while because he started off with the oldie about it being so dry that the Baptists were sprinkling and the Presbyterians were using a damp cloth. But then he added that the

Lutherans were passing out rain checks and at least one Catholic priest was working at turning wine back into water. With those new variations on an old theme, Russell walked away with the 1988 Grand Prize.

The second prize was doubled up, one going to Harlan Kroeger of rural Dannebrog for *his* remark about the drouth of '88. He said that he heard that things are much worse in North Dakota than Nebraska and so he decided to truck some of his cows up there just to show them how lucky they are.

Co-winner of the second-place award was Roy Stamm of Scotia, who protested, albeit weakly, that his story was actually true and not a lie at all, which would have been eligible for another award if it had come in the day before. Roy told the assembled crowd, estimated by Hall of Fame organizers at 1,455, that he had been having trouble with raccoons eating all of his sweet corn. He was told that he could discourage the nighttime raids by spreading newspapers around his garden, which he did. The next morning he came out and found a trio of raccoons eating sweet corn and reading the funny papers.

Honorable mention was awarded to the inevitable Anonymous Liar for his contribution, through radio KZ100 of Central City, to the effect that due to the drouth, Central City authorities had out-lawed water-skiing in the Platte River for the remainder of the summer of '88 because it was kicking up too much dust.

COLD WINTER, WINDY TALES

4

Okay, the summer of 1988 was one tough summer. And here we are, bracing ourselves for another tough winter. Darrell Nelson up in Oconto maintains that the weather around here is so tough, even the permanent residents live somewhere else.

Mearl Urwiller of Ravenna, just down the road from Dannebrog, sent along one goodie and promised several more. Promises, promises! I'm not even sure I believe the one he sent:

"I remember when I was a boy, we had a lot of snow early that winter. This was back in the days before we had any insulation of any kind or any furnaces at all. We heated our house with corncobs and wood-burning stoves.

"We had a lot of snow piled up on the roof on the south side of the house and the heat escaping through the roof caused the snow to melt even though it was so cold outside. This formed long icicles and they kept building up over the next few days.

"One morning when my mother got up—she usually got up first—there seemed to be a terrible draft. It seemed to be coming from up around the ceiling some place. When my dad got up she said, 'Find out where that draft is coming from. It's so cold in here.'

"After checking around, my dad found that the roof on the south side of the house seemed to be pushed up from the house, so he went outside to look and here these icicles had continued to build up through the night until they touched the ground and they were lifting the roof off the house.

"He got an ax and chopped them off so the roof could settle back down.

"Man, it was cold in there!"

And windy, too, Mearl. (Thanks for the good story, and I will be sending a book along to you just as soon as I can find one!)

Jim Smith of Decatur wrote me a while back that it was so cold at his place last winter that they ran out of propane and the only way they could keep from freezing was to open the refrigerator door and run it on defrost.

I have the feeling that the whole problem with Plains weather could be summed up and solved by an idea that Jerry Carlson of Genoa sent me some time ago. He writes that his buddy Cozmo Cown down at the C & D Repair Center finally had to set a rule on lying that you can only add on 20% to any story. It works pretty good and keeps your stories honest. Jerry says, "This way the story gets better each time it's repeated by someone else."

Only problem is, that some sort of thinking would put the Liar's Corner out of business and I would have to get an honest j . . . jo . . . jo . . . ! Well, you know.

WINTER MEANS FISH STORIES

5

December 10, 1988

Many of you long-time readers of the Liar's Corner know, during the winter I like to think about fishing. That's the best part about fishing—thinking about it. No fish to clean, no bait to stink up the refrigerator, no lines to untangle, no mosquitos. And all those lunkers that I dragged out of the river last summer. (Wonder why I can't find any of them in the freezer?)

Alex Kasha at the Skyline Ranch at North Platte insists that this is a true story. Do you believe him? I sure do.

"One Sunday morning it was so foggy we debated about going to church but finally decided to go. As we drove into North Platte we had to cross the bridge at the Fremont Slough. As we drove onto the bridge something hit the windsheild of our car. The fog was so thick it was impossible to tell what the object was, but when the second object hit my windshield I pulled to the side of the highway and stopped. I got out and found it was a large carp swimming across the highway in the dense fog. By then we decided it was too dangerous to proceed onto church, so I picked up the two big carp and drove back to the ranch. I got busy and cleaned the fish, and my wife cooked them for my dinner."

Speaking of fishermen, Jim Zuhlke from over at Sterling was telling me about his buddy Charlie, who reminds me of my buddy Sorry Charlie. Anyway, Jim's Charlie is retired and loves to fish. Jim asked Charlie's wife what he does in the wintertime when he can't fish. She told him he runs the bathtub full of water, puts on his breast waders, stands in the tub, and fishes in the sink.

Jim expressed some concern about the state of Charlie's mind (he does remind me of Sorry Charlie!), and he said that Charlie's wife really should have a doctor take a look at him.

She said they don't have time for a doctor. They're too busy cleaning fish.

"Smart" Aleck Arneson of Red Cloud complains that fishing hasn't been so good recently on the Republican. He writes, "Our creek dried up a while back and the fish—faced with extinction—grew legs and came up to the barnyard and ate with the chickens and hogs. Things were working real well for them until a cloudburst came up one day and the poor fish, having forgotten how to swim, all drowned."

'ORANGE' FENCE POSTS

6

January 1, 1989

As some of you know, Primrose Farm isn't really much of a farm. It's a tree farm, which means I do a lot more planting and watering than I do harvesting. But I do have a long and abiding interest in trees.

We plant mostly maple, ash, locust, and cedar but I did plow in a long row of hedge apples with the hope of getting some of those old-fashioned fence-post trees going along the road. It also gives the fellows up in town something to talk about: "Know what that crazy Welsch is up to now? Planting hedge apples! Hedge apples!!"

Well, the apples, as you old-timers remember, or orange, if you know them as osage orange, are great as bug repellants (you just toss them back into the corner of the closet or under the front porch), the limbs make terrific bows (the trees are also known as Bois D'Arc, French for "bow wood"), and the wood makes incomparable fence posts.

Ray Kubie of Lincoln sent a story that I used many years ago in a booklet I did for the State Forester's office, "Of Trees and Dreams." They used to say osage orange fence posts would out-last three postholes.

Another story about the infamous osage orange fence post is the one about the fellow who was bragging on and on about how much longer they last than other posts, until one of his buddies finally pinned him down: "Exactly how much longer will and osage orange post last than an oak post?"

Realizing that his credibility was about to be cast in doubt, the bragger thought the situation over for a moment and finally answered, "About 10 minutes longer."

I have stressed in many of my books that the fine art of lying prospered on the pioneer Plains, and was not restricted to the rough hombres of frontier communities. I just read through the 1924–25 Liar's Lair in the *Nebraska Farmer* and was struck again how, week after week, it was women who won the contest, and the final "champeen" was, as a matter of fact, a woman.

At any rate, ministers, too, have tossed in an extra grizzly now and then, as the phrase goes, as illustrated by the autobiography of George Barnes, written in 1885 and published by *Nebraska History* in 1946. The good Reverend Barnes reported, among other things, that cottonwood was about as twisty a wood as you would ever deal with.

He wrote that there "was one board in town that was so crooked it could not lay still on the ground, and one was told of one on a fence so warped that when a pig tried to get through into the cornfield, it came out on the same side it started in on."

STORIES FROM THE 'LOCALS'

7

January 21, 1989

About six or eight times a year, I tell you that the best stories are the ones I hear right around here—at Harriett's Cafe, in Eric's Tavern, or right around Lovely Linda's kitchen counter. I always tell you that because it's always true.

Just last evening Dee, Cathy and Bondo dropped by. The conversation took a nasty turn and pretty soon Dee, Cathy and Linda were all picking on poor Bondo.

In a desperate defense, Bondo muttered, "Okay, I have my weaknesses. But you've only seen one side of me."

"Yeah," Linda snorted. "The outside!"

Bruce Davis was in Eric's tavern the other morning and remarked that he had an idea how Eric could sell more coffee. "How's that?" asked Eric, already a little suspicious.

"Fill up the cups," growled Bruce, peering down into his.

Reminds me of Sorry Charlie. He spent thirty cents at Eric's for a cup of coffee a couple weeks ago—an event in itself—and just yesterday came back in for his fifteen-cent refill!

But then Sorry Charlie's idea of a hard day is having to deal the cards twice in one morning!

Now, I'm not one to doubt the representations of good Nebraskans, especially from one just up the road in Ord, but I do have my doubts about a letter from some guy named "Meese." Thad Meese of Ord says that he overheard two ranchers arguing about some rain they got. One said that he had gotten five inches of rain, and the second said that was nothing. He had gotten so much rain at his place that the water was two inches above the rain gauge. He was also growling that there wasn't enough wind turning his windmills to keep the stock tanks full. The second said, "Huh, not much wind! There wasn't enough wind to turn both windmills at once, so I had to turn one off!"

Finally, Dean Daubert, who advertises himself as my "favorite reader," an issue that my mother may dispute, sends me a story which he swears is the truth—a breech of ethics for the Liar's Corner. He says, "A friend of mine is really upset because he got a ticket for fishing without a license, and yet his neighbors are living together, and nobody bothers them.

Well, big deal, Dean. Bill Kloefkorn, Nebraska's State Poet, writes poetry without a poetic license and it is, after all, called a "lie-sense." I simply don't see what this has to do with being married or not. A bachelor, we all know, is a man who hasn't made the same mistake once, and let's recall for a moment what it was that Shakespeare said about women . . . whoops, that was Sherman and he said it about war.

STORIES TO SHORTEN THE WINTER

8

February 4, 1989

Well, I asked you to sit down and shorten the winter a little by writing me some good stories, and I guess you took my request to heart because I've been getting some good ones. I'll send out books to the folks who took the time to write me; if you send me a story and I use it in this column, I'll send you a book too, so hop to it!

Dan Chmiel, from just down the river at Fullerton, sent me a version of a story I first heard when I was working on my book on horse trading, *Mister, You Got Yourself a Horse.* Old-time horse traders, you know, prided themselves on being scrupulously honest. If anything was wrong with their horse, they would tell you about it. Of course you had to listen real close.

The way I heard it, the trader told the farmer, "Now this mare isn't very *good* looking, but she sure can pull." What the farmer didn't know is that she not only wasn't good looking, she didn't look at all: she was blind. And when you put her in harness, she *pulled* all right. Back, just as hard as she could!

Ron from Mesa, Arizona—he was too shy to send me his last name—told me that he used to move so fast coming home to meet a curfew as a Nebraska youngster that he would jump from his car and slam the door, run into the house, tear off his clothes, turn off the light switch, fluff up the pillow, and lay down his head—all before the room went dark.

And *then* he would hear the car door slam.

Betty Colgrove of Endicott responded for stories about hard times. She says that a welfare agent once stopped by a farm home to ask about the situation and the conversation went as follows:

Agent: Any savings?
Farmer: What's that?
Agent: Any debts?
Farmer: I owe everyone, have no credit.
Agent: Any back house rent?
Farmer: We don't even have a back house!

Gene Hoarty of Fairmont says that his mother worked hard during the thirties. They would catch a jackrabbit, his mother would make 50 gallons of jackrabbit stew—and they would still have the jackrabbit!

Leigh Fairhead sent in quite a story and if Leigh sends me an address, I'll send along a book. Leigh writes, "A friend and I were going through some cattle and as it happened we'd just implanted the calves with a new type of implant. My friend asked if we got the desired growth from the product and what we thought of it. I pointed out some trumpeter swans on a marsh nearby and asked my friend if he knew what they were.

"He replied that they were swans. I informed him that they were not swans at all but Leghorn chickens that I had tried some of those implants on.

"The only bad news I had to report was that it was awful hard to find their ears to implant them."

Leigh reports that this really did happen—and that friend went out and bought some implants for his stock, but she doesn't say whether that was cattle or chickens!

TRADING PICKUP TRUCKS

9

Elmo Sughroue over in Bartley tells a story that has a real moral to it. I'll just let you draw your own conclusions.

Last spring I went to a truck dealer to see if I could afford a new pickup. I hunted up my favorite salesman and I asked him to figure up what a ¾-ton pickup with a few extras would cost me.

These are the figures he gave me:

$10,671.00	Basic ¾-ton pickup chassis
740.00	350 h.p. V-8 engine
98.00	Four speed manual transmission
38.00	Optional axis ratio
92.74	Heavy duty 8-ply front tires
112.421	Heavy duty 8-ply mud and snow rear tires
56.00	Heavy duty battery
42.00	Gauges
48.00	Tinted glass
24.00	High power headlights
33.00	Dome light
52.00	Rear view mirror
268.00	AM/FM radio
56.00	34-gallon fuel tank
38.00	Two tow hooks—front
36.00	Heavy duty shocks
40.00	Heavy duty stabilizer
525.00	Freight
$12,970.16	TOTAL

The salesman then asked me if I had a trade-in and I said, "Yes, I have some cows I would like to trade for the truck."

"How much do you want for your cows?" he asked.

I said, "Well—

$500.00	Basic cow
45.00	Two-tone exterior
75.00	Extra stomach
64.00	Product storage area
90.00	Straw chopper
120.00	Four spigots @ $30.00 each
125.00	Cowhide exterior
45.00	Dual horns
48.00	Automatic fly-swatter
185.00	Fertilizer attachment
$1,297.00	per cow

" I guess I still owe you 16 cents," I said.

"My truck dealer still has the pickup and I still have my 10 cows."

I bought a pickup truck from my buddy, Bondo, for Linda for Christmas. I was sure that something was wrong with the transmission because when I put it on "R" it just sits there; on "N" it goes backwards; and on "D" nothing at all happens again, and on "2" it moves out, and fast.

When I asked Bondo about it, he explained, "R means 'Right where she sits,' N means 'Not forward,' D means 'Don't go,' and 2 means 'Too fast to stop 'er.' "

Well, I asked.

A LETTER MAILED BEFORE IT WAS WRITTEN

10

March 4, 1989

Sara A. Hansen of Blair, a friend of mine and of Dannebrog's for some time, writes to share with me a letter she received in 1944 from Dry Creek, just a couple miles from right here at Primrose Farm. For her trouble, I'll send her a book and an official membership in the National Liars Hall of Fame.

Here is the letter precisely as she received it:

Dear Sara,

I sat down, pencil in hand, to type you a letter. Excuse the pen.

I don't live where I used to live because I moved to where I live now. When you come to see me, you can ask where I live, because nobody knows.

I am sorry we are so far together; I wish we were closer apart. We are having more weather this year than we had last year.

My Aunt Nellie died and is doing fine and hope you are doing the same.

I started to Fremont to see you and I saw a sign that said, "This takes you to Fremont." I got on it and sat there for three hours but the old thing wouldn't move.

I am sending you a coat by mail. I cut the buttons off to make it lighter. (They're in the pocket).

If you don't get this letter, let me know and I will send it to you.

Our neighbor's baby swallowed some pins but they fed it a pin cushion, so everything is okay now.

Did you hear about your Uncle's accident on the bus the other night? He had his eyes on a seat and someone sat on them.

I would have sent you that $8 I owe you but I didn't think of it *until I sealed this envelope. I'll close now, because I have nothing to do but sit.*

Love, Mert.

P.S. Enclosed you will find a picture but for fear of losing it I didn't put it in.

NEAR AND 'DEER' WILDLIFE STORIES

11

March 18, 1989

We had robins down by the river during February when the temperatures were sub-zero. We had geese flying south in late February, about the same time other ones were heading back north. And, of course, there was that poor lost moose last fall. Strange things have been going on, all right, but then there were reports of weird things from all over the territories.

Terry Kublicek of Crete writes that he was having lots of trouble with deer on his place. He was about to order 20,000 bars of motel soap and two miles of rope to hang on the trees, just as recommended by the State Forester, but then he was uneasy about what everyone in town would say about that.

It was only after several weeks of continuing trouble that Terry figured out the problem: He would be out working on his tractor or doing chores and his wife, Kay, would call out to him, "Time for lunch, *Dear*," and even while he was walking in the door, all the deer in the county, thinking the call was for them, would also come running.

Terry says that he has asked his wife to use another term of "en-deer-ment," and he is now wondering if perhaps the problem he has been having with bees and rabbits around the place just might not stem from much the same situation.

Terry concludes that now he'll probably have to tell Kay that "Honey bunny" has to go, too.

Thanks, Terry. That explains a lot of the problems we've been having here at our place. So I have asked Lovely Linda to stop yelling, "Time for supper, you scruffy old coyote!"

Jim Farmer from Broken Bow writes that last summer Mason

City was having a Fourth of July celebration but the old cannon on the town square wouldn't fire. They went ahead with the program minus the boomer and at six that evening Clint Whitehead and Ivan Ferguson talked Ol' Jim into checking that cannon. Jim crawled into the barrel and could see that the problem was that they had left the firing tongs inside the chamber. Just then the charge went off and Jim went out over town. As he was coming down he could see that he was about to land in a patch of briars, so he quickly pulled out his pocket knife and cleared a 6- by 6-foot landing patch.

I'll bet Jim wishes his life were a little more like Warren Kempke's over in Blair, a lovely river town I lived in for a good many years. Warren claims that in Blair the old year went out so quietly last year that the New Year snuck in about 11 p.m.

Pfarmer Phil Pfeiffer pfrom north of Lincoln is even more pfamous pfor pfishing than he is pfor pfarming. He writes that he managed to get in a little ice fishing when things slowed down for him this past winter. He writes, "I caught a nice stringer of cubes . . . but you should have seen the *block* that got away!"

FOGGY TALES AND BEAVER DAMS

12

April 1, 1989

Claudeen Penry of Atkinson says that there is a woman in that town who works for her husband and he wouldn't give her any lunch break at all if it weren't for Paul Harvey and his 15-minute radio program. Claudeen thinks I should have a 15-minute radio show—because then this poor lady could have a half hour break. Ms. Penry's friend sounds a lot like Lovely Linda. Hmm.

The fog had been so heavy here at Primrose farm that the catfish have been coming up out of the Loup River to eat at our bird feeder. The ironweed has rusted, the dry ice is soggy, and the steel wool has shrunk three and a half sizes.

Ed Sejkora from Burchard writes, "We have some beaver dams on our place. One in particular would have high water one day and then the next day be low. Especially low when rain was forecast. One day I went down to check the dam. I discovered what they were doing. In some trash dumped off the bridge was two lengths of 6-inch stove pipe with a damper in it. The beaver were using this to control the water level by turning the damper."

Ed also maintains that the wind was blowing so hard that it blew the ear plugs out of his ears. It certainly didn't blow the wind out of him!

Gordon Stalder of Humbolt says that his neighbor was telling him about the cold weather in 1983. He said that it was so cold that if the thermometer would have been an inch longer, he would have frozen to death.

Lori Amico writes from Boston to comment on a story I did for my "Postcard from Nebraska" series on CBS's "Sunday Morning." Lori sends an article from a Boston newspaper about the current parking crunch there. Parking places, the writer complains, have been selling for $6,000 in Boston (yes, Nebraska readers, that's not a misprint—$6,000 for a parking place!), $8,000 in Beverly Hills, $10,000 in Marblehead, and indoor parking slots for $13,000 in Newburyport.

But now prices have soared, the newspaper writer goes on, to $101,000 last year on Beacon Hill, and most recently for $125,000.

Sounds great to me. The way I figure it, that makes my sixty acres worth something in the neighborhood of $87,667,922,654.33. If you're looking for a good investment, drop me a line and a blank check and I'll send you a couple of cheap parking places.

Bud Huges of Elkhorn says he recently heard of a politician who was so unpopular he ended up with minus six votes the last election. He says there's a friend of his there in Elkhorn who is so polite he says, "Excuse me," even before he belches. Now is that some kind of gentleman or what?

OF SPRING AND ROMANCE

13

April 15, 1989

In springtime a young man's fancy turns to love—at least that's what they tell me, and since spring is well along the way, romance is the topic for this issue of Liar's Corner.

I was the speaker for the Nebraska Democratic Party's Salute to the State Senators in February and I heard some marvelous new stories. My favorite was the one about the young fellow who picked up his girlfriend one cold night in Dodge, heading for the weekly dance in Howells, over in Lovely Linda's part of the country.

This smart gent made a point of having a nice carriage robe in the wagon and he and his lady cozied up for the long ride. Well, they snuggled, and kissed, and hugged the whole way, until when they were on the outskirts of Howells, the young lady said, "You know, I'm ready to go a little further if you are."

So the young man drove all the way to Clarkson.

I told that tale to Eric up at the Big Table Tavern and he said he was sure I was going to tell him the story from these parts, about the young fellow who was walking his girlfriend home to Nysted after a dance at Dannebrog's Pleasure Isle.

They stopped for a brief rest at a barn along the way and the young man asked his lady friend if he could have a little kiss. She said he could but there was a little problem in that she was about a foot taller than he was. So he stood up on an anvil there in the barn and got his kiss.

They walked on another mile and again the young man asked for a kiss, and the lady allowed as how he could have one. Another mile and another kiss, and so on until they reached her father's home.

Well, I have only two things to ask now," smiled the eager swain. "First, can I have one more goodnight kiss, and second, I wonder if you'd mind if I left the anvil here?"

Bruce Davis, one of Howard County's accomplished storytellers, often tells about his first date with his wife, Annette. "If I grab you and hug you and kiss you, will you yell for help?" he says he asked her.

"Only if I think you need it," he maintains she responded.

INQUIRING MINDS FIND OUT

15

May 6, 1989

Imagine for a moment what it was like around Primrose Farm the middle of March when folks were calling from all over the country asking, "Have you seen the article about you in the *National Enquirer?*"

Well, we hadn't, and Lovely Linda was scared half to death that the *Enquirer* had maybe linked me romantically with Vanna White. I, on the other hand, was fairly certain that the story was probably about me cozying up to Sweet Allis, my 1937 tractor.

As it turned out, *you* were in the *Enquirer!* Thank goodness they didn't use any names but they had somehow latched onto the best of your stories in last year's Liar's Hall of Fame awards ceremony and republished them.

So, if you have ever wondered if the *Enquirer* publishes the truth . . . well, we now know that it *does* publish lies!

It's been a long time since I picked on lawyers, maybe too long. I cleared this story with the Nebraska's Big Kahuna Lawyer, Attorney General Bob Spire (no kidding, I did!) and he laughed hard enough that it's probably okay to go ahead and share it with you.

Arnold Buhr of Filley played it safe and blamed the story on his pal Ed Aden of Wymore. I don't know why, but Arnold added that Ed is a bartender at the Wymore Legion Club—and is employed at the city's waste treatment plant. I don't know if that information is supposed to make the following more believable or less, but here goes anyway.

According to Arnold, according to Ed, a nice young couple was en route to the church for their wedding when they were involved in a terrible automobile accident and they were both killed. They arrived at the Pearly Gates and informed St. Peter that they would still like to be married. St. Peter said that he would work on it.

One hundred years later the couple came back to St. Peter and he said that he was still working on the problem. So they waited another 100 years and went to visit with St. Peter again. St. Peter said, "I haven't forgotten you but I am still working on a little problem."

Well, the couple waited another 100 years and once again made the trip across Heaven to see St. Peter. This time St. Peter said, "It's all taken care of. You can get married tomorrow."

The groom said, "We've waited 300 years now and to tell you the truth, I've noticed that some really nice young ladies have entered the Pearly Gates during the past three centuries. St. Peter, if things don't work out so well for us, is there a possibility that we might be able to get a divorce up here in Heaven?"

St. Peter frowned and said, "Well, I doubt it. We've waited 300 years for a preacher, so who knows how long it's going to be before we can ever get two lawyers up here to handle the divorce!"

IT'S ALL IN THE TIMING

15

May 20, 1989

There's probably a rule against this but the winner of the book award for this issue of the Liar's Corner is my old man, Chris Welsch. Maybe instead of a book, I'll offer not to show up for a meal at his table for a month or so and save him a couple hundred dollars.

But his story is good enough that, relative of yours truly or not, I have to pass it along to you.

Here goes:

There was a farmer who had a section of land and his farmstead was in one corner of that section.

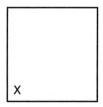

Every morning he set off around his section to check his fences, to make sure no cattle were out, to make sure the irrigation was going according to schedule, and so forth. It took him exactly one hour and 20 minutes to cover side A of his section.

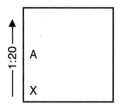

And it took him exactly one hour and 20 minutes to cover leg B of his daily route.

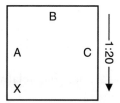

To no one's surprise, it also took him an hour and 20 minutes to cover side C of the section.

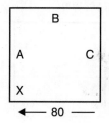

But the real poser is that the last side of the square, the one that returned him to his home, took only 80 minutes.

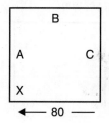

Can anyone figure out why? I couldn't. And I suppose that's why I'm no longer at the University.

Thanks, Pop!

TALES THAT KEEP POPPING UP

16

June 3, 1989

The most common story submitted in the *Nebraska Farmer*'s original tall-tale contest in 1924 was the one about the day it was so hot the popcorn popped right on the stalk; two mules in the next field saw that popcorn on the ground, thought it was snow, and froze to death.

That is still by far and away the most common tale sent to this column, averaging, I suppose, about two entries a month. Isn't it amazing how much life a tale like that has. Sixty-five years and still going strong.

Well, there are other stories, too, that pop up around here with amazing regularity and vitality. One that has been making the rounds over the past 5–10 years is the one about the fellow who approaches a farmer about buying his old mule, explaining that he is going to hold a raffle up in town and the mule is going to be the prize.

The huckster says he'll be back the next week with $50 to pay for the mule, and sure enough, the next week down the road he comes, his pockets stuffed full of dollar bills he has gathered up in his very successful raffle operation.

The only problem, the farmer explains to him sadly, is that the mule has died during the intervening week. "I don't suppose you'll want to buy a dead mule," the farmer frowns.

"No problem," the raffle operator says, as he smiles and peels off $50 to pay the farmer for the dead mule.

"But aren't you going to get a lot of complaints about raffling off a dead mule?" the farmer asked, amazed.

"Only one, I guess," says the slickster. "That'll be from the guy who won the raffle, and I'll just give him back his dollar."

I don't know why that story makes me think of the State Legislature but it sure does.

Arnold Kyhn of Boelus solved a mystery for me last week. He explained patiently that they don't raise longhorns in Minnesota because the critters kept getting their horns caught in all the trees. Then the trees grow so fast the animals are lifted up 50 feet or so off the ground.

Arnold says that sometimes you can still see those skulls high in the trees, or even the remains of the whole animals.

One of the nice things about living out here in the country is that whenever you have a question, all you have to do is ask and someone is bound to have an answer.

Sally Finck was circulating a petition the other day to get someone to do something about the pilot she said was flying around over Dannebrog and spitting. Someone finally told her that that was a rain sprinkle and gradually she remembered the old days when it used to rain around here.

"Never mind," she said and tore up her petition.

THOSE 'TALL TALES' DAYS OF SUMMER

17

June 17, 1989

I think summer is now officially on the way so we can look back and laugh at winter. Maybe. Harlan Johnson, Newman Grove, writes that the mercury dropped so fast at his place in February it actually bent the nail that held the thermometer on the barn wall.

But summer is coming and we should keep in mind such stories as the one Fred Hansen sent me from Wausa. It was so hot one summer up that way that when he left a log chain laying out in the yard, he came back from his lunch break to find that it had crawled off into the shade of the tractor.

Fred Schroeder of Shelton sent along a story that he swears is the truth and I, for one, believe him. He says that he and his wife, Maxine, vacation winters in the South—a pretty sissy thing to do, if you ask me—and that on every trip they pick up a few desert rocks to spruce up their yard there in Sheldon. Last summer when they returned from their sojourn in the gentler climes, Fred says he noticed some of his desert rocks were smaller than he recalled.

He checked closer and they seemed to be wrinkled up, a little like prunes or raisins. Well, he decided to clean them up a little so he put them in a bucket of water and started scrubbing them when Maxine called him to lunch.

He forgot about the rocks in the bucket, but when he checked a couple days later, he found that the rocks had swelled up enough to break the bucket. Fred theorizes that here in this dry Nebraska climate, the desert rocks had simply dehydrated. Jim Dageforde of Richmond, Va., writes that his father was a good storyteller and used to say that during the thirties it sometimes rained ducks in

Nebraska. Seems the dust would pile up on their wings, they would fly through a cloud, the dust would turn to mud, and " . . . down they would come!"

And I have received a bumper crop of mail from readers (notably and in this case the book winner, Doug Knehans from Guide Rock) complaining that it just doesn't seem fair that they work so hard to come up with Plains tall tales for the Liar's Corner and then Bruce Watson sweeps the field with his "Weather Report" in the March 18 *Nebraska Farmer* in which he predicted that it would be abnormally wet in Nebraska through March and April.

COLUMNS DRAW PECULIAR LOGIC

18

I guess the theme of this Liar's Corner is "Mixed Reactions," because I'm passing along responses to previous columns and they reflect some peculiar forms of logic.

For example, my spring column on romance inspired Beth Gibbons of Crawford to send along her favorite romantic poem:

> *I climbed the door and shut off the stairs.*
> *I said my shoes and took off my prayers.*
> *I brushed my makeup and set my sheets.*
> *I shut off the bed and climbed into the light.*
> *And all because he kissed me good night.*

The March 4 edition of the Liar's Corner was made up in large part of an amusing letter received by Sara Hansen of Blair in 1944. Mrs. D.E. Haussler of Arapahoe writes that she, too, received a similar letter, and she sent a copy to the Liar's Corner. It is obviously the same kind of humor but with almost completely different material.

I get the feeling that such letters might have been a common form of humor in the past. Whatever the case, the comic letters are still fun today, and here is Mrs. Haussler's letter for your funny bone:

Dear Son,

Just a few lines to let you know that I'm still alive. I'm writing this letter slowly because I know that you cannot read fast. You won't know the house when you come home . . . we've moved.

About your father . . . he has a lovely new job. He has 500 people under him. He is cutting the grass at the cemetery.

There was a washing machine in the new house when we moved in but it isn't working too good. Last week I put 14 shirts into it, pulled the chain, and haven't seen the shirts since.

Your sister Mary had a baby this morning. I haven't found out yet whether it is a boy or a girl, so I don't know whether you're an aunt or uncle.

Your Uncle Dick drowned last week in a vat of whiskey in the Dublin brewery. Some of his workmates jumped in to save him but he fought them off bravely. We cremated his body and it took three days to put out the fire.

Your father didn't have much to drink at Christmas. I put a bottle of castor oil in his pint of beer and it kept him going until New Year's Day. I went to the doctor on Thursday and your father came with me. The doctor put a small tube in my mouth to take my temperature and told me not to open it for ten minutes. Your father offered to buy the tube from him.

It rained twice last week. First for three days and then for four days. Monday was so windy that one of our chickens laid the same egg four times.

We had a letter yesterday from the undertaker. He said if the last installment wasn't paid on your grandmother within seven days, up she comes.

Signed, Your Loving Mother
P.S. I was going to send you ten dollars but I had already sealed the envelope.

And Lillian Kingston of Arcadia finally dropped me a note. She says that she has been wanting to for some time but has had to wait until now so she could save up enough spit to seal the envelope!

NO 'ADG' FOR STORYTELLERS

19

July 15, 1989

Summer is in full swing. We've had a little bit of rain, and so around here it's been a little easier to laugh over the past few weeks.

For example, Eric over at the tavern reports seeing a sign in St. Paul that posed the lofty philosophical question, "How did they measure hailstones before they had golf balls?"

And Lovely Linda read some place that veterinarians have been reporting an increasing problem among Nebraska cattle with a problem labeled ADG. The article went on to explain that ADG is "Ain't Doing Good."

Bruce Rundle of Hastings sent in the old story as told by his father, Dan, about the fellow who was picking corn so fast that when he dropped an ear and went back to pick it up, he accidentally grabbed his own overshoes, shucked them off, and threw them into the wagon. He continues that he stood up and was then hit on the head by the last three ears he had thrown.

Now, I've heard that much of the story 50 times before but then Bruce continues on that on the one occasion his grandfather, Bill Gronewold, listened to this tale and was obviously unimpressed. "I'll bet two of those ears," he sniffed, "were on the side of his head!"

And that is a new one on me!

Marion Tacher of Grand Island writes that he wanted to write to me at my *Nebraska Farmer* office but didn't have the address in our new digs. Well, my suite is on the 27th floor of the *Farmer* offices and there's no way you can get into my office without first getting past my six secretaries and chauffeur.

Marion is serving as a reporter, sending on a tale from Tannies

Waller of Grand Island. When he was a boy living near Holdrege, Marion writes Tannies had to plow fields for his father, using a team of mules. The mules had been trained to work until the noon whistle blew in the nearby town. At that point they would stop, knowing it was lunch time. One day, at about 9:30 a.m., the quiet was disturbed by the whistle of a work train approaching a crossing north of the field and the mules stopped in their tracks, believing it to be noon and time to eat and rest.

Tannies finally had to take out his watch and show them that it was only 9:30 a.m. before he could get them to complete the morning's work.

Marion goes on that at first he didn't believe Tannies but when he told him that he had once walked three miles to school and three miles back in a wagon wheel track his doubts were allayed: This man had to be on the *straight and narrow*.

Me, I'm not so sure. I never met a mule that needed a watch to tell the time of day!

PROFOUND QUOTATIONS

20

August 5, 1989

Lyle Fries is our mailman. He says that he is going to go into business this year with Dwayne Berger. Lyle says that he and Dwayne aren't sure what they'll be doing in the new business but they just can't resist the temptation of hanging up their shingle: "Berger and Fries."

Most of the contributions for the Liar's Corner come to me by way of Lyle when he delivers my mail, but last week I ran into Frank Marsh, an old friend, at the Omaha airport. We were both on the dead run and so only had time to exchange a couple of quick lines. I forget what I said to Frank, but he stopped me dead with his bit of folk wisdom.

"Roger," he said sternly, putting his hand on my shoulder, "just remember that it is better to have loved a short girl than never to have loved at all." (Say it slowly, or quickly if you want, several times and it will make more sense).

Then I flew to Utah where another friend reminded me of the wise words of Ray Lum, an eastern mule trader now gone to the livery stable in the sky. He said, "You live and you learn." Then he paused and added, "Then you die and forget it all."

Mrs. W. G. Holm of Lincoln wrote to remind me of the salesman who stopped at a neighbor's house when they lived in the Sandhills. He asked directions and was told that he should go down the Sandhills road, if you can call it that, about a mile and a half to a fork in the road and then take either fork because he'd just get lost anyway.

Oh, by the way, thanks to the *Nebraskaland* magazine for bringing its readers notice to the latest product of the National

Liars Hall of Fame, our extra fancy combination stinkbait and sandwich spread. My friend Dan Selden has tried it out and says it's as good as dynamite. Not for fishing, for eating!

HOT WEATHER TALES

21

August 19, 1989

As you can imagine, being a contributing editor of the *Nebraska Farmer* carries a lot of responsibility with it, but when I come home after spending another 12 or 15 hours working on the next Liar's Corner, I am content that I have added another brick to man's "Mansion of Wisdom."

But the one thing does bother me about this heady position of mine: I just can't answer all of your letters. I apologize for that. A lot of the stories I have used before—this column has been running for four years now. Some I have used before in my many books, and some I tuck into files from where they may not appear again for as long as a year or two.

Moreover, I get mail from readers of my columns in other publications, from folks who have enjoyed my books, from television fans, people who are looking for information and various collection agencies, but please understand that I very much appreciate your kindness in writing. While I may not be able to answer every letter, I sure do *read* them all.

This week's mail contained some goodies. Clayton Gillespie of Dalton claims that it was so dry out in the Panhandle that he actually saw ducks trying to swim in a mirage on a highway!

Bud Hughes of Elkhorn says he came from a small town. "I asked the local publisher how such a small town could support a newspaper. He said to cut costs he prints the same news every week. He can do this, he explains, because no one in town can read."

Bud continues, "Of course I had to ask why they would take the paper if they can't read. The publisher answered with yet another question: 'Who wants his neighbor to know he can't read?' "

Bud adds a story about a friend of his who was about to freeze to death last winter when he saved his life with quick thinking—he put the thermometer into some hot water and it quickly read 110 degrees F. in the shade.

Bud maintains that he reads my stuff but I think that's another lie because he asks, "Why are most liars men?" Bud, every major lying contest in the country, including the one in 1924 that started this column, has been won by a woman.

How old are you anyway?!

Gene McIntyre down in Arizona says he's 56. Big deal. He also says that during the thirties his mother told the kids to walk with their arms outstretched so they wouldn't fall down the huge cracks in the farm yard. So if he's so tough, what's he doing in Arizona?

An old friend, Dave Demler of Ohio but occasionally from Dannebrog, wrote, "I thought I got ½ inch of rain in my gauge Tuesday but I looked down and there was a bug in it. I removed the bug . . . and found I only had a ¼ inch."

POINTS FOR K-STATE FOOTBALL

22

September 2, 1989

You can tell autumn is finally on its way: The temperature is getting cooler, the politics are getting hotter the days are getting shorter—and my columns are getting longer.

And the sounds of football are in the air, especially *jokes* about football. Edvert Aden of Wymore sent me a football story, for example. Now, I am not the least bit interested in football, which puts me decidedly in a minority in Nebraska, but I'll have to admit Edvert's story is worth six points:

"A K-State fan took his dog to a K-State game, but the tickets were sold out so he went downtown in Manhattan to find a tavern that allowed a dog to come in. He found one and settled in to watch the game and when K-State made a field goal, the dog ran out into the center of the floor and did three backward somersaults. The bartender said, "Wow, that's amazing! What's the dog do when they make a touchdown?"

"I don't know," the man replied, "I've only owned him five years."

And speaking of pets, George Mohr of Hawthorne, Calif. (What kind of lies can someone from *California* tell?!) claims he once owned a cat that swallowed a ball of yarn. The next litter of five kittens, he writes, was born with sweaters on.

He also says he once had a dog so mean that he had to explain to neighbors that that dog was actually an alligator—he cut off his tail and painted him yellow.

And he says that once he walked by the hen house and heard cackles that sounded a lot like "Ouch! Ouch!" Upon investigating he found that the hens were laying square eggs.

Probably because he fed them a square meal that day.

I'll probably get into trouble for picking on Kansas again but, hey, I simply report what folks send to me. I don't make this stuff up!

Jan O'Keeffe of Overland Park, Kan., writes that she recently spent a night in Hays and was afraid to go to sleep because of the blowing dust. She was afraid she'd wake up in Oklahoma. A fear worthy of consideration these days, I'd say.

She also sent along a tearsheet from the *Kansas City Star* in which Joe Stephens reports that Vernon Deines said his crop was so bad this year he is trading in his combine for a lawn mower. I'm trading my lawn mower in for tweezers.

Theresa Tansen writes from Newman Grove to tell me that her father, John Potmesil, is a liar. Well, that's a nice thing to say about your father, Theresa. She says that last winter it was so cold, he maintains he had to use jumper cables on his wheelbarrow to get it started. Well, what's dishonest about that? It was his wheelbarrow, wasn't it?

Mrs. Arvon Jensen lives in Grand Island but her husband grew up right across the river from Primrose Farm. I guess he moved south for the scenery. Anyway, Mrs. Jensen writes, ". . . We used to have fogs around here—when it used to rain—and the fogs were so thick, the road signs were in braille." I've been wondering what all those little holes in the traffic signs are!

AN ASSORTMENT OF
'TRUE' STORIES

23

Well, it's getting along toward harvest and I think I've done
pretty well this year, considering. In my line of work, even if it
doesn't rain, I can count on a bumper crop of *corn*.

Art Flammang sent me a letter he wrote in December, which
must be some sort of record for procrastination. Not only was the
letter old, but so were the jokes. Art previously sent me a story,
you may recall, about his grandfather's axe. Well, he adds to that
the old-timer about the clock so old that the pendulum's shadow
had worn a grove in the back of the clock's case.

Then he tried to redeem himself from that old clinker by passing off the antique story about being chased by a bull and jumping
for a branch 30 feet off the ground, missing it on the way up but
catching it on the way down.

As if that were not enough, Art went on to tell the story I have
used in several of my books about the hog that ate a case of dynamite and was kicked by the family mule. The punchline usually
goes that the mule died, the barn was blown over and the hog was
sick for a week.

But Art does add a nice little filip to that tale. He maintains that
a few weeks later, a piece of his pitchfork handle came down—
autographed by two Russians and a Frenchman.

Get it? Astronauts? The handle went that high? Aw, forget it.

Bob Teichert lives in Denver but reads the *Nebraska Farmer*. Is
that legal? Anyway, he writes, "Last summer I was driving in the
North Platte area. It was a hot day and a hot wind was blowing.
The humidity was way up there. I'll tell you what—the air was so

thick and the wind was so hot, a pheasant hen flew across the road and laid an egg—and it hatched before it got to the road."

I thought that was pretty funny but I got no pleasure at all from his next callous remark that folks over 50 have one thing to be grateful for—after a shower the mirror is steamed over. Lovely Linda thinks that's a hilarious line. I don't.

You'd be amazed at how many of the letters I get start off, "Now, this is a true story." Sure it is! Take this gem from Mary Lou McCracken of Red Cloud: "Now, this is a true story. When I was a child I was helping my grandmother gather eggs. It was a hot, humid afternoon and the nests in the chicken house were made of orange crates. There were always a lot of knotholes in orange crates and a snake had been in one of the hen's nests, swallowing an egg. It crawled through a knothole into the adjoining nest and swallowed another egg and now he was stuck, not able to get out either way."

I probably would have doubted Mary Lou's word about that one but she went on to say such nice things about my "Sunday Morning" appearances on CBS that it became obvious to me that this lady's word is as good as gold.

J. Gordon Olson, just down the Loup River in Genoa, writes that he overheard a couple of truckers on the CB radio not long ago and one was complaining about his wife's cooking. He said that he caught her throwing eggs down the garbage disposal. When he asked her what was going on, she explained that she was throwing away the "spoiled" eggs, the ones "that had turned brown."

Boy, she is dumb! The brown ones are the *chocolate* eggs! Even I know that.

DRY HUMOR FOR RELIEF

24

October 7, 1989

I know that some of the Plains have received plenty of rain, and even too much, but for the third summer in a row Primrose Farm has toasted and dried in the sun and we sat here watching our trees die. About the only thing that has kept us going is the good hot-and-dry stories readers have been sending us, and which we now present to you.

Aaron Peters writes from Scribner that it is so dry that way, the other day when he came in from the fields and tried to top off his gallon jug of water, it took *two* gallons to fill it up.

He also says that when he gets out of the tub the bottom looks like a dried-up creek bed because even the water is drying out. My mom and dad used to fill in some of the erosion gullies in our south forty with the settlin's from my weekly bath. Only problem was, nothing would grow for seven years or more.

Gilbert Wolbbecke of Pleasant Dale writes, "One of those days when it was 106 degrees I was out cultivating. After three or four hours riding this open tractor without an umbrella, I stopped at the end of the field and decided to walk down to the ol' fishing hole and cool off. It's amazing how hot the water was. I didn't see any fish. I walked up the creek bank back to the tractor and there they were, lying on the bank in the shade panting. Now that's hot!"

Edwin Bredemeier of Steinhauer—and if you're a *real* Nebraskan you know how to pronounce that—says that he got into an argument with a Texan about who has the hottest weather. Well, the Texan said that sometimes it gets hot enough down there to fry an egg on the sidewalk. "Big deal," snorted Edwin, as he dropped a whole egg from a building about six stories high so it would land and break "over easy." Unfortunately, the wind caught that egg and blew it two blocks into a pasture near the town—a hard-boiled egg!

Ray Harpham, a champeen liar, says that last summer was so tough down Holstein way that when the wind blew across his empty rain gauge, it played "How Dry I Am."

Morris Palle lives in Blair now but his family came from Denmark in 1910 and settled—where else—one mile north of Nebraska's Danish Capital, Dannebrog. (I got a letter last week from some folks in California who are planning to visit Dannebrog next year. They wrote that they hope to visit the "nice cafe in the *downtown* area of Dannebrog!" Are they going to get a surprise!)

Morris writes, "One morning us boys got up and all the sows were in the potato patch. They were going down the rows like a lister. We got them back in the pen, finished chores, and went off to school. Next morning, same thing: All the old sows were out again in the potatoes. They had dug up two rows and were sitting waiting for the gravy.

THISTLE-PURPLE CORNHUSKERS

25

October 21, 1989

Now that summer is pretty much out of the way and things have cooled off a touch, we can start to laugh a little bit more enthusiastically about it. Here's the latest mailbag full of hot-and-dry stories to cross my desk.

Fern Sigler of Ravenna writes that her nephew Jerry Jakob wrote to her from Tucson. He maintains that they had a sunstorm down there last winter and the wind piled up sunshine on the driveway so bad that he had to shovel it out of the way just to get to work.

Jerry, don't you know it's not nice to lie to your Aunt Fern?!

Allen Madsen of Nehawka says it was so hot in that area this past summer that once when they had a little rain shower he went out to check to see how much they had gotten and found that the rain gauge was still so hot the water in it was boiling.

Our problem in central and eastern Nebraska is musk thistle. And I am ready to do my part to solve the problem. I have three suggestions:

1. I read someplace that camels love to eat thistles. Prehistoric camels did just fine in what is now Nebraska, so we should just import about 50,000 camels and let them feast on thistles.

2. Then we can declare thistle-purple the new color for the Cornhuskers. People will be selling thistles outside Memorial Stadium for $5 a piece, Husker fans (who will buy anything) will buy them, and that will cut into the thistle problem pretty good.

3. We will take out ads in east and west coast newspapers with the warning that we will no longer tolerate the illegal harvest of musk thistles in Nebraska. We'll put up billboards urging people

to call the thistle hotline whenever they spot illegal thistle harvesters. Before we know it, every thistle between Missouri and the Rockies will be up in smoke.

Lyra Johnson dropped us a note, saying that their Thompson Creek pasture north of Riverton is so pretty that it is a pleasure digging thistles there. Hey, Lyra, our place here on the Loup is gorgeous, so bring your shovel and machete and have at it!

Anyway, Lyra (nice name!) writes, "On the way back to the pickup our 6-year-old, Libby, wanted to carry the spade. I gladly let her. Along the way she stopped and started digging up a thistle. I told her we didn't have to dig those because they are Canadian thistles. She looked at me with a puzzled look on her face and asked, 'When are they going to come and dig up their thistles?' "

Good idea, Libby. Then we can get the Russians to take back their thistles, the Japanese their beetles, the Germans their measles, and the Dutch their elm disease, and most of our problems would be solved.

TALL TALE HIGHS AND LOWS

26

November 4, 1989

I've never met Arthur Benson of Springfield, but he must be an interesting fellow. He says that the other day he was flying home over Wyoming; the plane was so high, Arthur says, even his uncles looked like aunts.

As if that weren't bad enough, he writes, "When I was a little boy, my mother told me to put on a clean pair of socks every morning, but at the end of the week I couldn't get my shoes on."

Irvin Wagner over in Franklin writes that the drouth has been bad there. In fact, he says, "The milo is so poor, the wild turkeys are eating it out of the combine bin faster than we can combine it."

While I was on the road last week, some kind soul passed along to me the real secret of succeeding in the farming business: "Roll with the punches and keep your wife working."

Alice and Will Ronspies of Pierce had a visit from their 6-year-old grandson—from London, England. A highlight of the visit was the moment when the child almost touched a calf on the family farm. One thing puzzled the boy, however. "Grandma," he asked Alice, "why are the mommies selling all their calves?"

When asked why he thought they were for sale, he explained that all of them had sale tags in their ears!

Ken Ryan of Greely said that he prayed all year that the drouth would break so he would be able to shut off the wells and take the boat out to do some fishing.

His prayer was answered and, after Labor Day weekend, he had to use his boat to get out to the wells to shut them off.

Ken says, "I'd better be careful how hard I pray the next time."

Lovely Linda finally got to the point in her prayers that she was giving specific directions to the farm since the Big Rainmaker seemed to be off about three miles in every direction.

Jack Wachter of Herman says that no matter how much rain he gets, his lying neighbors always say they got more. The only way he can keep up with them, he complains is to put up two rain gauges!

I was told a story a couple weeks ago about one of the cruelest hoaxes I have ever heard. A community not far from here had one of those impossible people who always have a few more hundredths in the gauge than everyone else.

Well, some jokers who drove by this fellow's house early every morning on their way to town, stopped at the guy's mailbox and added first a couple hundredths to the gauge, and then a couple inches. Before long, the rain stretcher was getting three inches in his gauge when everyone else was getting only a trace.

The jokers said they think he finally quit bragging about his rain readings when someone pointed out to him that he had had over 16 inches of rain in one week and his lane wasn't even wet!

SNAKES AND MILK

27

November 18, 1989

Claude Goddard of Haxtun, Colorado, says that Haxtun is almost as good as being in Nebraska, and sometimes when the wind blows just right, the state line bends enough to put him 15 to 30 feet on the north side of the line. He says he was a witness to a struggle between a bullsnake and a rattlesnake. Each got the other's tail in its mouth and proceeded to swallow all it could. Pretty soon, he maintains the two just disappeared and to this day he doesn't know who won the fight.

Reminds me of why hoopsnakes became extinct—males roll clockwise, females clockwise, and, well, you know.

Bernard and Meneda Phifer of Mason City write that things were so tough in the Mason City area this past summer that their friends, Tom and Shirley Sellman, carried little red flags on wires on their windrower. They used them to mark the windrows so the baler knew where to go.

Donna Kucera over in Palmer says it was so hot there in Merrick County this past summer that their shop furnace kept coming on. Why? Well, the thermostat was set at 65 degrees and the darned thing was trying to cool the place down from 110 degrees!

What I liked most about Donna's note is that she says the Liar's Corner is the first thing she reads when her copy of the *Nebraska Farmer* arrives. She says her husband Bill's philosophy is: "Life is uncertain, so eat dessert first."

George Haynes writes from Ogallala that he ran a grade B dairy for years and had a yearling that the hired man's kid started fooling around with when she was only a yearling. "I be danged if she didn't give milk," George writes. "She would fill a 16-quart bucket twice a day. We milked her for 11 years and she never did freshen. Never had a calf in her life. I guess it was kind of in the breeding, because her mother got started giving milk the very same way and she never had a calf, either."

Veldon Johnson in Spencer says that his pal Joe Milacek had to hay some steep hills in order to get enough hay for the winter. One hill was so steep, he says, Joe upset a four-section drag. He claims that one day he actually say a herd of cows chasing a gopher that had a blade of grass in its mouth.

LIARS' ANNUAL RECOGNITION

28

It is the custom about this time of the year every year to announce the winning lies for the previous year and the inductees into the National Liars Hall of Fame. Here goes:

A celebrity-packed, black-shirt-and-white-tie crowd cheered the honorees at the 65th annual awards banquet of the National Liars Hall of Fame in the Dannebrog Convention Center, October 31. The 2,000 in attendance agreed that veracity had never taken such a beating during a non-election year as it did during the now-classic awards ceremony at the National Liars Hall of Fame Convention Center.

The gala day began with the first ever Formula One Grand Prix Race in the streets of Dannebrog, with the favorites—Andretti, Unser, and Sullivan—finishing first, second, and third. Fred Andretti expressed his appreciation and said it sure was worth driving over from Grand Island for the event but he had expected something more than a $5 off a bearing pack over at Mel's Sinclair and a warm six-pack of Mountain Dew. Gaylord Unser and Lumir Sullivan, second and third place winners, filed protests with race officials, claiming that Andretti repeatedly rolled through stop signs during the race.

Both said, however, that they would be back next year when the green flag drops from the front porch of Harriett's Danish Cafe.

At the evening awards banquet the institutional award for the best tall tale of the year went to the *Des Moines Register* for its report of the Iowa farmer who prided himself on having his corn knee-high by the Fourth of July and was doubly proud last summer was knee-high twice before the Fourth—once on the way up and once on the way down.

Bill Orr, husband of Nebraska Governor Kay Orr, won the Mendacity Diplomacy Award. He notified officials at the Hall of Fame that he would not be able to attend next year's Hall of Fame Awards Dinner because, "I have an important funeral to attend that day."

The late Jim Knapp, Kearney attorney, won the Karma Award for his naming of the three things necessary to become a successful trial lawyer—"Sincerity, sincerity, sincerity." Jim said that once you learn how to fake that, you can get away with almost anything.

The annual Pinocchio Awards for 1989 are:

Third Place: Bud Hughes, Elkhorn. "A fellow I know has a radio so old he could still get 'The National Barn Dance' on it."

Second Place: Bondo Adams of Boelus, who took one look at my new windvane and said, "That thing's no good for Nebraska. It only points one direction at a time."

First Place: Maxine Christensen, Anita, Iowa, who has a 1979 Dodge car with over 200,000 miles on it. She claims that it's so old, "the license bureau now issues upper and lower plates for it."

Named to the National Liars Hall of Fame for 1989 was Otis Hulett, founder of the Burlington, Wis., Liars Contest, one of the major factors in the preservation of competitive prevarication in America during this century.

Roger Welsch, founder and director of the National Liars Hall of Fame, said, "Hulett was a liar. A damned good one, too."

CORN, MELONS AND 'SAGE' VIEWS

29

January 6, 1990

Once things settled down in town after the hubbub of the National Liars Hall of Fame Awards Banquet, I had some time to sit down with my Dannebrog buddies and find out how things were going with them.

Bruce Christensen said he had to clean out an old grain bin and the corn was so full of weevils, they were carrying the stuff back into the bin faster than he could auger it out.

And I think I may have gotten a hint why things are so tough on the farm scene these days: farmers are still too easygoing. I had a chance to sample some of Bill Fries' popcorn and it was so good, I asked him if I could maybe buy 100 pounds or so from him.

"How long have you lived here?" he asked, looking at me as if I were some kind of nut. "Are you a tourist or are you just too lazy to go out into my field and steal it like everyone else?"

So my folks and I spent a nice afternoon picking ears of popcorn from Bill's field, and I think I found out something important—stolen popcorn, just like stolen watermelon, tastes a lot better than the stuff you buy in the store.

Like good ol' Rod Hat used to say, "Nothing improves the taste of a watermelon like the smell of gunpowder."

Let's see what's in the Primrose Farm mailbox! Cecil McMullen of McGregor, Texas, maintains that he has developed a perfect watermelon: the seeds grow on the outside like corn on the cob, and all you have to do before you cut it is wipe it off.

Mrs. Victor Lutkemeier of Hastings says the late Henry Lutkemeier used to take issue with the idea that when you start any job, you should always begin at the bottom. "Not in digging postholes," he insisted.

Todd Walton of Verdigre, the heart of Kolache Kountry, poses a philosophical dilemma in his note to the Liars Corner: "When you go to your local convenience store that is open 24 hours a day, 365 days a year, why do they have locks on the doors?"

Lud Petracek—and there's a Czech name for you!—of Bridgeton, Missouri, says that in the old days there were all sorts of spot removers on the market—some left a ring, some couldn't be used on silk, some were dangerously flammable, some poisonous. But his grandmother brought over a spot remover from the Old Country that never failed and had no such faults. She called her secret device "scissors."

Fran Kreutz of Hastings says that one fellow in this community thinks that bacteria is the rear entrance to the cafeteria. He maintains that this fellow and his brother started a bank with their own money and after they had loaned all their money out, they skipped town. He says there is one town near Hastings that is so small it doesn't have any public restrooms, just pay bushes.

OVERALLS AND THREE-PIECE SUITS

30

The wind was blowing so hard here at Primrose Farm yesterday that our asphalt parking pad was peeling up at the northwest corner, but that cold wind was nothing compared to the hot air that blew when Lyle the Mailman brought in the day's supply of mail shortly after noon.

There was a letter from Delores Colburn of Valentine, and Delores is my kind of lady. She says she likes my jaunty appearance when I wear my overalls on my segments of CBS's "Sunday Morning."

You'd be amazed at the number of nasty letters I get from swells in Lincoln and Omaha who think its absolutely dreadful that I give the impression there are people in Nebraska who wear overalls and farm for a living. "Why," these uptowners huff, "here in Nebraska we're just like the tony folks in New York City and Los Angeles, what with fancy places to eat, art stuff piled along the Interstate, and dressing-for-success. You make us look like a bunch of hicks."

You see, these drizzles think I wear overalls on the show just to be cute. Well, I wear overalls because they're the most comfortable, most useful, most handsome clothes I can imagine. I'm wearing 'em as I write these very words; I'll be wearing them tomorrow, and I'll be wearing them on Hallelujah Morning, just you wait and see.

The only folks who wear three-piece suits these days are politicians, defendants, and politicians who are defendants. I've met somewhere in the neighborhood of 187,664 dishonest people wearing business suits. On the other hand, a few years ago I met a guy in overalls who lied to me about the size of a catfish he once caught. Give me hicks in overalls every time.

Anyway, I started telling you about Delores Colburn. She says she's been ranching for over 50 years, which means she started when she was 2. (A 61-year-old once told me he'd been farming for 60 years. "What'd you do for the first five years?" I laughed. "Milked and spread manure," he snapped back.)

Anyway, Delores says she has a hard time these days separating the truth from the fiction. The wind blew the leaves off her apple tree the other day and before she could get out into the yard to rake them up, the wind changed and blew them right back up on the tree.

She continues, "On my way to Grand Island, I toured the beautiful downtown Dannebrog and saw the golf course. I'll bet when Arnold Palmer saw your piece on CBS "Sunday Morning" he went into depression. I've never seen a golf course he designed with so much character—either in the course or in the players."

Maybe I should explain for the three people in Nebraska who didn't see that piece that the Dannebrog Country Club course is also a pasture, where several dozen head of cattle graze while the duffers make divots. On the Dannebrog golf course, the words "chip shot" take on a whole new meaning! Stop by and play a round sometime if you think you can afford the $2 fee!

I got a lot of items from Dave Harmon, and over the next couple weeks I'll be passing them along to you. For example: "My uncle recently took out a fire-insurance policy on his new barn. As he signed the application, he said to the insurance agent, 'If my barn was to burn down tonight, what would I get?' "

" 'About 10 years,' the insurance man said!' "

SPINNING A FEW COWBOY YARNS

31

February 3, 1990

In the last Liar's Corner, I teased you with a couple from Dave Harmon, who must be quite a storyteller and is welcome anytime at the National Liars Hall of Fame in Dannebrog.

He writes, for example, that two young boys visiting a dude ranch were playing cowboy. They brought their imaginary steeds to a halt in front of the packing box that was serving as the Last Change Saloon. The older lad swaggered up, pounded on the bar, and growled, "I'll have rye."

The second boy, who was much younger, imitated the older boy's swagger, and piped out from under his oversized hat, "I'll have whole wheat."

Dave tends toward cowboy stories, I guess. He says a California youngster, in the country for the first time, rushed home to his mother and said, "I've seen a man who makes horses. He had one nearly finished when I saw him. He was just nailing on its back feet."

One more Dave Harmon tale: A penny pinching cowboy went into a tack shop and asked to buy one spur. "What use is one spur?" asked the proprietor. "Well," the cowboy replied, "I figure if I can get one side of the horse to go, the other side is likely to come right along."

I started reading Mrs. Andrew Jacox's letter from Lincoln and I'll have to admit, she really had me going—"Thought I'd tell you about the hog my son raised. We lived near Interstate 80 and one day my teenage son Les came home with a young pig he'd found along the highway. The pig had jumped or fallen out of a truck or trailer apparently. He wasn't hurt much—skinned up a little and his tail was snapped off—but Les put him in a pen with some water and feed and the pig made himself right at home.

"In a few months the pig was ready for market and Les took him to a sale, but Les came home and told me he'd had to sell the pig wholesale . . . Because he couldn't *re-tail* him!"

I'm not sure if I have the next story right. Eric Nielsen, up at the Big Table Tavern, was asking me if I had heard about the scientific experiment the University hosted last year.

Eric says the University gave three groups—one made up of Germans, one of Japanese, and the third of Nebraska farmers—each a silver ball and a copper ball and told them that they had one year to manufacture something out of those basic materials. Eric says at the end of the year, the Japanese had produced a remarkable new computer out of their two lumps of metal. The Germans had manufactured a radically advanced armored personnel carrier. The farmers? Well, they looked at one another, shrugged their shoulders, and admitted that they had broken one of the balls and lost the other.

The reason I'm not sure I got the story right is that I broke one of the pencils I usually carry with me to write down such tales, and the other one . . . well, you get the idea.

RAIN, SPUDS AND COWBOYS

32

date??

I've been down with the flu and a cold for a good month. Antonia has been sick, too, and then the furnace quit on us. So I asked Plumber Dan to take a look at it, which he did. He got out his tools, dug down into the bowels of the machine, stood up, dusted off his hands, and said, "Yep."

"Figure out what's wrong with it?" I asked, somewhat encouraged.

"Sure did," said Plumber Dan. "It doesn't work."

I was cheered up, however, by a package that came my way. It came to me through a roundabout route so I managed to lose the name and address of the wise Nebraskan who sent it, but it's too good not to pass along to you, even without the proper footnotes. It is, of course, a Nebraska rain gauge—a spent .22 caliber cartridge! But if it's so darn funny, why is it I'm not laughing?

Steve Wolverton of Madison says the Alpine Cafe in Madison is a great place to pick up stories because "at some time during every day, except Sunday, it has at least one liar in attendance."

Steve continues, "A couple of years back the fellas were discussing their potato-growing skills. 'Frosty' McCallum announced that his potatoes were so large and heavy that he couldn't lift them and had to tip a 5-gallon bucket on its side and roll them in so he could carry them home.

Stan Kellsen, our local used cow dealer, quipped, "That's nothing. My spuds are so big that after digging 'em I had to hire Adolph Long and his dump truck to bring in two loads of dirt just to fill in the holes!"

Steve says that Frosty just turned 80 and isn't giving up on topping Madison's other spud nuts. He recently said that he had to use a backhoe to dig his potatoes this year.

Over the past few issues of the Liar's Corner I've been passing along stories shared with us by Dave Harmon. Dave tends toward cowboy stories. For example:

First dude ranch cowboy: Why did you get a dachshund?

Second dude ranch cowboy: Another cowboy told me to get a long little doggie.

And . . .

Cowboy: What happened to your hand?

Dude: I put it in the horse's mouth to see how many teeth it has.

Cowboy: And?

Dude: And the horse closed its mouth to see how many fingers I have.

But one of my favorites from Dave's recent collection is the following:

The wife of a small-time sheep rancher near Montrose, Colorado, was dyeing a tablecloth a bright blue color in a vat in the yard when a little lamb fell in. Sometime later a passing motorist saw the blue lamb and offered the rancher $100 for it.

Thinking he might have a good thing going, the rancher dyed more lambs and sure enough, they sold quickly at a good profit. "Soon," the rancher later told his friends, "I was dyeing the lambs every color of the rainbow—pink, lavender, yellow, green. They sold just as fast as I could dye them.

"And now I'm the biggest lamb dyer in the country!"

I don't know for sure why, but somehow that story just fits fine in this particular space, don't you think?

ALL BECAUSE OF A SNAKE

33

March 3, 1990

Frances Neiman of Thedford sent me this story, but frankly I don't believe it. It sounds to me too much like business-as-usual at Primrose Farm! Here goes, anyway:

This fellow was explaining why he was in the hospital. He says his wife had brought some potted plants into the house to keep them from freezing, not spotting a little green snake hidden in one of them. When the snake warmed up, it slithered out and went under the sofa. The fellow's wife saw it and screamed bloody murder.

He was taking a bath at the time. He leaped out of the tub and ran naked to see what the screaming was about. She told him a snake was under the sofa, so he got down on the floor to look for it. Along came his dog and cold-nosed him. He thought it was the snake and he fainted.

His wife though he had a heart attack and called an ambulance. The attendants rushed in and loaded him on the stretcher and started carrying him out.

About that time the snake came out from under the sofa. The ambulance men saw it and dropped the stretcher and broke the fellow's leg (which is why he was in the hospital).

Her husband, on the way to the hospital with a broken leg and a snake under the couch, the wife went next door to enlist the aid of a neighbor who had the reputation of being an outdoorsman, having camped out with the Cub Scouts last summer. Armed with a rolled-up newspaper, he took a few swishes under the couch and decided the snake had left the premises.

"Thank goodness," sighed the woman, plopping down on the

couch. Her hand dropped between the cushions and brushed against a scaly skin, which she immediately realized was the snake.

Screaming, she fainted dead away in the sofa and the snake slithered quickly back under the couch. The great hunter drew upon his meager first-aid skills, recalling a demonstration of mouth-to-mouth resuscitation he had seen.

So he pushed the woman's head into the proper position but just as he started the first breath, in ran his wife—having heard her neighbor's scream—with a sackful of groceries in her arms. Seeing her husband mouth-to-mouth with the neighbor woman on the sofa, the neighbor's wife slammed the sack full of canned goods across the top of her husband's head. The crash and scattering cans brought the fainted woman up with a start.

When she saw the man lying on the floor and his wife bending over him, she was sure he had been bitten by the snake so she ran to the kitchen and brought our a small bottle of brandy, which she began to pour down the fellow's throat.

His wife, regretting hitting him with the sack, wrestled the bottle away from the well-meaning woman, sloshing booze on both of them in the process.

About that time, two policemen summoned by a neighbor who had heard all the commotion, walked in. Everyone was talking at once, trying to explain how a snake had caused the whole mess, but the officers, smelling the brandy, had their doubts.

The policemen left with a summoned ambulance, containing the unconscious husband and his sobbing wife, which took them away to the hospital, leaving the first woman completely unbalanced, and a small and very frightened snake under the sofa.

See? Just another day at Primrose Farm.

A DIFFERENT TYPE OF FISHING STORY

34

March 17, 1990

I think winter is beginning to get to some of the folks here in Howard County. A couple of days ago I overheard the following conversation up at Eric's Big Table Tavern.

Plumber Dan: Hey, Russell, who's that Jerry who's always in here drinking coffee about 11 o'clock?

Russell: I don't know. What's her last name?

Pfavorite Pfarmer Phil Pfeiffer pfrom Lincoln wrote me the following narrative: "I drilled a hole in the pond to go fishing. Before I could bait my hook, it froze shut again. So I had to drill another hole, and so on till finally I hit the bottom. It wasn't until late spring that the hole thawed a little and by summer it had been so dry that the pond dried up and the darn hole fell over and just about hit me while I was hoeing weeds one hot day. I walked over to get a piece of ice to cool off with but shortly after it hit the ground it turned to steam, which just made me all the hotter."

I know that's a lie because Phil never hoed weeds in his life!

Jo Riedy writes a fine column in the *Cairo Record* entitled "Dig a Little Deeper." It highlights stories from the past in our local area, something I always enjoy. I took special pleasure in a piece she found in a 1922 issue of the *Record.* With the permission of Jo and the *Record,* I reprint that item here:

"Charlie Harris of Texas, in the printing business, got peeved at a doctor who wanted bids on several thousand letterheads, different sizes, different grades, and different colors. As Charlie wrote, 'Am in the market for bids on one operation for appendicitis . . . 1-, 2-, or 5-inch incision, with or without ether, with or without nurse. If appendix is found to be sound, want quotation to include putting same back and canceling order. If removed, successful bidder is expected to hold incision open for about 60 days as I expect to be in the market for gall stones, and want to save extra cost of cutting.'"

This reminds me of an actual event in these parts recently when a farm family made an emergency run to the hospital to have a son's cut taken care of. The doctor spent about two minutes making three stitches and charged the farmer $75, which he paid on the spot and without complaint.

As if to prove that there is a god, two weeks later that same farmer was out working in the fields and a hunter slid off the gravel into a muddy ditch, where the car became firmly embedded. The farmer went over to the car with his tractor to give the fellow a pull, and whom do you suppose he found driving that car? That's right: the doctor.

And what do you think it cost the doctor for that tow out of the ditch? You got it! $75.

I still have some tales from Dave Harmon's recent letter. I hope you like 'em because I sure do!

He asks, "Do you know what you get if you give your heifers hysterectomies? Decaffeinated cows."

Maybe the following one is too close to home for comfort: "I dream of making a fortune farming, just like my father," the young man sighed.

"Your father made a fortune farming?" his friend asked with some surprise.

"No, but he sure *dreamed* about making a fortune farming."

DANCING, HUNTING AND HAY POLES

35

April 7, 1990

Well, I wish I had another forty pages of Dave Harmon's stories, but I'm down to the last two, and here they are:

"My uncle always worked on cattle ranches and was a stranger to traffic in the big city. One day while driving in downtown Denver, he pulled into line behind another car at a red light. When the light changed, the woman in the car ahead did not respond. After waiting a bit, he called out politely, 'Ma'am, if you're going to homestead, better get closer to water.' "

"A Colorado rancher decided to visit his daughter and her family in Chicago one summer. During his visit, his teenage grandchildren had a dance party. After watching the action silently for 20 minutes, the rancher laid down his pipe, turned to his son-in-law and said, 'If that don't bring rain, nothing will.' "

That might be worth a try around these parts. This winter even the snow has been so dry that Lovely Linda just sweeps the stuff up and tosses it into the fireplace. Only a little at a time of course because otherwise it might burn too fast and burn out the chimney.

Mildred Anderson of Polk, one of the prettiest towns in this whole state of pretty towns, is 84 years old and anyone who would call her a liar is going to have to deal with me personally. She wants one of my books, and by golly, she's gonna get one. She writes the following from her own personal experience!

A neighbor of hers went out for a load of hay. Having no poles to put on top of the hay to hold it on to the wagon, he took his ax and commenced to chop down a stalk of corn from his field nearby. He had it almost cut in two when one of the seven ears on the stalk fell from the stalk, crushing him to the ground. It broke his neck and one of his legs. He would have died but for the health-giving properties of the good Nebraska climate, which made him well again before he had walked half way home.

Hmmm. I wonder if Mildred is really 84 years old. I wonder if she is really form Polk. I wonder . . . well, never mind. But she is definitely in line for the Liars Hall of Fame Awards next fall!

Dennis Adams of urban Boelus won second prize this past year and he isn't giving up on first prize for next year. Dennis was out hunting with Plumber Dan and they stopped at a farm house to ask about the game situation. "Oh, there are quite a few bunches of quail out there," the farmer enthused, so Dan and Dennis took out across the field, their 4-gauge shotguns over their shoulders.

A few hours later they came back, pretty well worn out and with their game bags empty. "Well, boys, how did you do?" the farmer asked.

"We saw some of your bunches of quail," Dennis grumped. "A couple of bunches had one quail a piece and the rest had less than that."

THE WHOLE STORY ON HOLES

36

Larry Fraas from over at Lodgepole sent me quite a story, one that seems particularly appropriate for a spring column. He says, "Our soil is so hard that the prairie dogs pull up their holes and take them with them when they move.

"Two years ago we had a sudden spring blizzard that caught many prairie dogs moving holes. The holes blew onto the roads and drifted full of snow. We couldn't break through the drifts, so had to wait for them to melt. The melting of course filled the holes with water and made for muddy roads. It was nearly a month before out dust storms filled the holes and made it possible to get to the coffee shop.

"During that month I almost got around to doing some work, and that was scary."

Now, that alone would have won Larry the book that I sent him but as far as I'm concerned, the real prize-winner is a cap he sent along with his note. On the front it says proudly, "FRAAS FARMS" . . . and then in smaller letters, "but not very well!"

I spoke recently to the St Paul and Dannebrog Co-ops and a nice lady stopped me as I left the building and told me that her father used to tell a story about the fellow who was at an auction and bought a mule, mostly because no one else was bidding on him and this fellow felt sorry for the bedraggled beast.

He got the mule as far as home but simply could not get him to go into the barn. Every time the farmer tried to lead the mule through the door, the mule's ears would hit the top of the door and the mule backed off, in no uncertain terms.

The farmer let the mule stand out in the yard all night and the next day started again the laborious process of trying to drag the mule through the doorway. A friend dropped by and watched this struggle for a half hour or so. The farmer tried to tie the mule's ears down, to back him through the door, to cover his eyes, but nothing worked.

The visiting neighbor finally offered, "Look, why don't you take a shovel and dig about six inches out at the sill of that door?"

"Well, you darn fool," the new owner of the mule sputtered, "I'm having trouble with his ears, not his feet!"

Speaking of mule stories, Gene Meyers dropped us a note from O'Neill, bragging about how smart the folks are up his way in Irish country. He writes, "This farmer passed away and left his estate to his three sons. Among his possessions he had 17 cows and his will stated everything should be divided according to the need of each son, so he left the youngest half of the cows, the middle son a third, and the oldest a ninth. Now the complications began because they could not figure out how to divide the uneven number of cows without killing one and cutting it up. They needed the livestock and really didn't want to butcher one but as much as they argued and figured, they couldn't come up with any way to sort things out.

"Finally a neighbor came along riding a mule. He stopped and listened to the discussion for a while, finally saying that he would help them with the situation. He was a very smart man—probably one of my relatives. He said they could have his mule and they put him in the pen with the cows so now they had 18 head, and they commenced dividing them.

"A half—nine—went to the youngest son, a third—six—to the next, and a ninth—to the last, eldest son, making a total of 17 cows. The mule was left standing there, so the man took him back and rode on out of the farmyard."

Wish everything was that easy.

A TRAIL OF TALES

37

Bud Hughes won an award in the 1989 National Liars Hall of Fame awards for his story about a radio so old it still got the National Barn Dance.

Bud writes that it is one of the nicest awards he never got. What Bud doesn't understand is that the award is being engraved and will shortly be on its way. Hey, we may be liars down at the Hall of Fame but we are not pikers.

Anyway, Bud says it's almost as nice as the time he won the slow reading award at his school there in Elkhorn. He says that the school wasn't all that great anyway. He writes, "A sign in front of the school said, 'Slow School Children.' One student, in his seventh year of high school, was asked why he was so persistent. He answered, 'I was planning to go to college.'

"Part of the problem was the faculty. The coach was fat and out of shape, the music teacher lisped, the English teacher spoke with an accent, and the home ec teacher couldn't boil water. And they were the good ones."

Now, this story from Glenn and Wilma Preston of Lyons (Get that? Ly'ens?!) is one of those you have to think about for a few seconds before you say, "I don't get it." Take it from me: This is a funny story. It's in the running for the 1990 Liars Hall of Fame awards:

An elderly couple, in their 90s, went over to the lawyer to get a divorce. The lawyer asked why they waited so long. They said, "We wanted to wait till all the kids were gone."

Cal Dahlke writes me that already this spring he has been watching the robins pulling worms out of his yard and the noticed that the wind was blowing so hard they were having a hard time keeping their stability. Moreover, he could see that the robins were landing and staying in one place.

His binoculars helped him figure out the mystery: When the robins landed, the worms would come out of the ground and hold them down so they wouldn't blow away.

Mike O'Brien of Grafton wrote to me ages ago about a story that appeared in the Liar's Corner. He says he was glad to read about Gene Hoarty's jackrabbit stew—I reported that she would make 50 gallons from a single jackrabbit and still have the jackrabbit.

Mike writes, "Many times I was fortunate to partake of that stew. It was so thin it only would weigh two pounds per gallon and when a dust storm blew through you could eat it without opening your mouth."

Gilbert Wolbbecke of Pleasant Dale reminds us on the hot days of last summer, which all too soon we'll be feeling again: "One day when it was 106 degrees, I was out cultivating. After three or four hours of riding an open tractor without an umbrella, I stopped on the end and decided to walk down to the ol' fishing hole and cool off. It's amazing how hot the water was. I didn't see any fish. I walked up the creek bank back to the tractor and there they were, lying on the bank in the shade, panting. Now that's hot!"

WHEAT WOES

38

Ken Laux sends the following gem from Hastings, for which he'll be getting a copy of one of my best-selling books (well, my mom bought a bunch anyway):

A farmer walked into his banker's office and asked, "With the farm economy so bad, I don't suppose you would loan me any money to get my winter wheat in the ground, would you?" The farmer had a good net worth and a good performance history on other loans so the banker said, "Sure."

After the farmer got the loan, the farm economy got even worse and the banker thought he better drive by the farmer's field just to keep an eye on his collateral.

The wheat was in, had sufficient moisture and looked good, so the banker drove to the farmer's house thinking they would have an optimistic conversation about the prospects of a good crop.

"That wheat sure looks good," the banker said.

"Yeah, but the winterkill will probably do a good part of it in," said the farmer.

Next spring the banker drove by the farmer's field and the crop had come through the winter in excellent shape.

The banker stopped once again to visit with the farmer.

"Well, if the Hessian fly or grasshoppers don't get it, we'll probably have a hailstorm just before harvest," the farmer commented.

The banker shook his head and went back to his office.

He returned to the field about the middle of July and saw some of the lushest stubble he had seen for years. Knowing that nothing else could happen to the crop, the banker went to the farmer's house again to have the first optimistic conversation he had managed to get out of the farmer since he had loaned him the money to plant the crop.

"I drove by your wheat field just now and from the looks of the stubble I'd guess that wheat made at least 50 bushels to the acre," the banker said with enthusiasm.

"Sure," said the farmer. "But do you realize what a crop like that can do to the land?!"

WIND, HOLES IN THESE STORIES

39

June 2, 1990

Spring is here in full force, and in Nebraska that force can be something! One day when tornados were tap-dancing round Primrose Farm, I was reminded of one of my favorite old-time stories about the time a farmer was out in his front yard practicing his tuba when a tornado came along and drilled him eight feet into the ground.

Norval Marks, a Nebraska exile in Iowa, writes: "Having grown up in Valley County, I thought I had endured the strongest and fiercest winds to be found anywhere in the country. Not true. This past winter, while in the Rio Grande Valley of Texas, I found out what really strong winds are all about. Horseshoe players throwing against the wind found their shoes coming back like boomerangs. The really good players became adept at throwing reverse ringers, which they referred to as "boomer-ringers."

Marvin Schlueter of Hardy reports on one occasion this past winter a couple of old-timers at the Byron coffee shop heard that ice fishing was really good, so they thought they would give it a shot. Well, they went, but they weren't having much luck, so one of them made his way over to some other fishermen who seemed to be having some luck. He thought maybe he could find out what they were using for bait.

When he got back and sat down, his buddy asked, "What did you find out?"

"For one thing," the first codger responded, "they cut a hole in the ice."

The next time these two whiz-geezers were at the coffee shop, they were so enthusiastic about their adventures that two more locals decided to give this ice fishing thing a try. "Be sure to cut a hole in the ice," one of the first pair warned, whereupon the other two laughed, "How dumb do you think we are?!"

They weren't so enthusiastic when they returned that evening and reported that by the time they got a hole cut in the ice big enough for the boat, it was time to come home.

David Stevens of Wausa is a little tired of all the complaining about the harvest last fall. He says he and his neighbors thought everything was just hunkydory because when they were combining it worked out that they only had to get loaded every Saturday night. He says he really likes the monitors in the new combines that tell you when the grain tank is full but all he needed was a calendar in the cab.

Herman Ostry of Bruno writes that he would send me a story but his neighbors are already looking at him funny, a logic I can understand, especially if you consider the next item on my desk.

Ol' Bud Hughes, a veteran of the Liar's Corner, reminds me that there is a big hill at the east edge of Dawson: "One day the curbside regulars noticed one of their compatriots running down the hill full tilt. 'Old Deek sure is feeling spunky this morning,' one remarked.

" 'Nah,' the other corrected. 'He's just too lazy to hold back.' "

TORNADOES, A GREENHORN AND RATS

40

July 7, 1990

I sure was glad to hear from Harry Hanson, the fiddlin' wheat farmer from up north in Gordon and one of my favorite story-tellers. Harry says that during a recent rash of tornadoes, one picked up all the buildings on one farm, including the windmill. Harry says they found the windmill standing perfectly upright about four miles away, still pumping water.

Lawrence Sexson from Farnam writes about an experience he had when he was a wrangler in the Sandhills. He says that his crew stopped on one occasion at a windmill and stock tank to get a drink of water and a greenhorn to the group stepped over a nearby hill to take care of a call of nature. "He had not been gone long before he came yelling that a rattlesnake had bitten him on his left buttock. Well, the greenhorn ran about a half a mile before one of the boys riding a quarterhorse managed to run him down, rope him, and bring him back to the windmill."

They managed to get him hogtied, lanced the bite with a pocketknife, and drew out the poison in the well-known, decid-edly unpleasant manner and after he calmed down a little, the greenhorn stepped back over the hill to try again. "Darned if here he didn't come again, whooping and hollering, dancing and prancing. The boys roped him and brought him in again and this time the foreman took a closer look at the wound.

"Let me tell you something about the West, boy," the grizzled veteran drawled. "The next time you step out into the bushes on one of those chores, it'd be a good idea to take off your spurs!"

One of my favorite storytellers, Darrell Nelson of Oconto, says he entertains himself by reading the Kansas State Board of Agriculture reports from the early part of the century, which says a lot either about night life in Oconto or how far along in years ol' Darrell is getting. Anyway, he says he thinks he discovered a tall tale buried right there in the official reports, on page 696 of the 1911 biennial report, masquerading as a news story. I'll let you judge for yourself:

"After an investigation covering two weeks, William Krohback has learned the reason he has been receiving only two or three eggs a day from his flock of 60 hens, and incidentally found something. This morning he saw two big rats in the act off making away with a newly laid egg. One of the rodents was lying flat on its back with the egg tightly clutched in its four paws while the other rat was dragging it along by the tail. Krohback was so impressed by the sight that he watched the rodents for three minutes, during which time they carried the egg for 20 yards along the fence until they came to a hole in the ground, into which they took the egg. One of the rats became tired while carrying the egg and changed placed with its fellow rat. [from *Poultry* magazine]"

Eugene Stevens of Sumner says that last summer it was so hot, dry and dusty that the fish in the streams in his part of the country were swimming backwards to keep the dust out of their eyes.

THE VALUE OF HOT AIR

41

August 4, 1990

I love it when I get stories from the ladies. I don't know why it is, but they do seem to be the best. Mrs. Everett Vollbrecht writes from Columbus that a friend of hers is a checker in a local grocery store and was telling her that one day she was checking groceries and, as usual, she blew some air into the plastic bag before she put some grapes in it, to keep them from being squashed. Before she could ring up the weight and charges, the customer's husband said, "Now you can let the air out of that bag and weigh it again for the correct weight! I am not paying for air."

Of course the checker did what she was told, what with the customer always being right.

Ray Johnson over at the Dannebrog grocery store always makes sure I don't blow into the produce bags; he read somewhere that hot air is lighter than regular air.

Steve Harris over at Jack's Bean Company (now, how's that for a great company title?!) wrote a nice letter to the Liar's Corner. I listened to folks in the western part of this state talk about "dreadable" beans for years before I figured out they weren't talking about beans that one should be afraid of but "dry, edible" beans!

Now it turns out I may have been right in the first place. Steve says they finally had to fire one of their employees over at the Grant plant where they pack their beans. Seems one of their best customers died of an incurable case of the hiccups because this careless employee was putting the brans in the bags upside down.

Burl Baxter and Mort McBride from up at Ainsworth wrote, asking for some free advertising for a new product of theirs, and since I do what I can to support Nebraska industry, I am glad to do that. Burl and Mort write, "The soil is hard out at Burl Baxter's hog ranch but we have arrived at a solution to help the hogs root. May be ordered from Burl or Mort, Rural Route, Nebraska."

Burl and Mort say you can test your need for one of their Wrought Iron Rooters by trying to drive a nail into your soil; if the nail bends, then you should probably go ahead and order one rooter for every ten hogs. (Before you try to fashion one for your hogs in your own shop, you should take note that these quick fellows have a patent pending.)

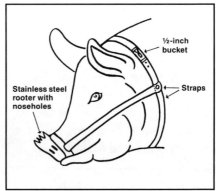

An illustration of how the Wrought Iron Rooter is fitted over the hog's head

½-inch bucket

Straps

Stainless steel rooter with noseholes

BLARNEY FROM O'NEILL

42

August 18, 1990

There must be a lot of storytellers up in O'Neill. I get a lot of letters from up there, most recently a long letter from Harvey Tompkins (he didn't give me his return address so I can't send him a book) of that fair city. He says that the bottom ground along the Elkhorn River used to be pretty rich and grew some great corn: "The farmers had to keep their team of horses on the trot to keep the corn planter from running over the new little corn plants."

Harvey says that in early immigrant days a couple of Irishmen were fresh in O'Neill from the Auld Sod and just as they got off the train, an old-fashioned fire wagon came roaring by with smoke and sparks flying out the top and men running along side. It must have been some fire, because pretty soom, here came two more. "Well, will you look at that," said the one Irishman to the other. "They're moving Hell and three loads have gone by already!"

Ken Messmand, a *champeen* storyteller from the grand metropolis of Chester, writes: "A group of farmers were gathered in town on a Saturday afternoon, as farmers did in those days, and they were bragging about their teams—which one could pull the biggest load, which one could start the biggest load, which one had the most staying power, and on and on. Finally, they noticed that one old graybeard sitting in the corner hadn't said a word. One of those present finally said, 'Mr. Sykes, you haven't said a thing about your horses. Didn't you ever have a good pulling team?'

"Mr. Sykes shifted his chaw, studied a moment, and replied, 'I never had a team that could pull your hat off, but I had the backing-uppinest team you ever saw. They once backed two tons of coal. Up a flight of stairs. On a harrow.' "

Now, that's the way the liars used to operate in the good old days!

An anonymus friend stopped me as I was passing through a Nebraska town one day and told me about a farmer who went to his friendly banker and said, "I've got bad news and good news."

"Let me have it," said the banker.

"Well, the bad news is that I didn't have a crop again this year."

The banker sat there for a minute or two and then asked, "So what's the good news?"

"Well," smiled the farmer, "I'm going to stick with you one more year!"

Glen Stewart of Albion writes that he went out one day last summer to view his withering crops. His dog went along with him and, as dogs will do, took the opportunity to relieve himself at the end of one corn row. Well, Glen says, it was so dry that when the dog finished, every stalk of corn in that 80-rod-long row was at the end of the row.

Glen says it was about that time, too, that the heat melted the nails in his barn and all the siding slid down, piling up neatly at the base of each wall. Worst of all, Glen couldn't get his barn repaired by winter. It was so cold he had to take his cows into the basement for 3 days to thaw out their bags.

And even then he couldn't sell the results as ice milk because at that time of year the cows hadn't been out in the pasture for some time and, of course, the government insists that all dairy products be "pasturized."

Elsie L. Florea of Sargent sends material from the repertoire of a master storyteller, John Hance. Hance's story is about a tourist at the Grand Canyon who looked over the rim. "The day was damp and he had on a pair of rubber boots. He leaned out a little too far and fell over. He was able to keep an upright position, so when he struck the bottom, he bounced. Naturally he came up past the rim again. This bounce was repeated several times, but he was never able to grab hold of the rim. 'In the end,' John said, 'we had to shoot him to keep him from starving to dxeath.' "

TO TELL THE TRUTH

43

September 1, 1990

Every now and again I devote one of these columns to the truth and, folks, this is one of those times.

I was visiting up at Eric's Tavern a few weeks ago—just to see what time it was, of course—and Eric pointed over at Sorry Charlie and says, "Now there's a guy who wouldn't pay a nickel to see an earthquake." Which had me baffled because I'm not sure I would pay a nickel to see an earthquake. But, anyway, Eric is one of the reasons I like small-town life.

I cannot for the life of me imagine where his funny lines come from, and I get the feeling that sometimes he isn't all that sure himself. A couple days ago I was sitting with Eric, having a cup of coffee, when a little old lady walked up to us and asked, "How do you get to the cemetery?" "Grab your chest and fall on the floor," Eric said without so much as a smile. (I almost said, "dead-panned.") I folded up in laughter but the little old lady seemed unimpressed. She said, "Well, I haven't been in Dannebrog for 17 years now and so many things have changed."

"Well, we moved the cafe," said Eric, "and we moved the grocery store and the post office, but so far we haven't moved the cemetery."

The lady left without, I think, catching a single one of Eric's zingers.

Then we got into a conversation about the doctor up in Michigan who invented a suicide machine. Eric put the whole flap-doodle into perspective for me when he remarked, "I don't get it. I've been doing the same thing with my potato salad for years and no one said a word about it." I went home and ate something out of the fridge.

My sister-in-law, Lisa, is just learning about small towns. She moved out here to Howard County from Phoenix, Arizona, a few months ago. The other night, lightning struck an electrical transformer near her house and she's a little on the nervous side anyway, so she called up a neighbor, who is a fireman, and screamed into the phone: "Dan, lightning just struck the transformer in front of my house!"

"That's okay," Dan mumbled sleepily. "REA will be out to fix it in the morning."

"But the trees and the pole are on fire," Lisa hollered, not in the least calmed.

"That's okay," tried Dan again. "The rain will put it out." And, of course, it did.

Small towns are full of such things; if you keep your ears open, it's a laugh a minute. A friend commented to me the other day that he had seen a store sign in another small town reading, "We buy junk, we sell antiques," but my favorite one that popped up recently, is: "We cheat the other guy and pass the savings on to you."

And that's the way things work here, too. I may fib now and then to others, but for you, it's nothing but the truth!

ALLIGATORS, TO BOOT

44

Wonder if I'll ever get used to living out here in the boondocks. I can't believe half the characters I run into on a daily basis. For example, Sorry Charlie is the cheapest man in the county; they say he is so cheap he's never spent a week and won't pay attention.

But Sorry Charlie is also the surliest guy I know. He came into the tavern the other day, grumbling and growling, and someone asked him what his problem was this time. "Can't you see?" he snarled, pointing out the window at the rain hitting the street.

"So what? It's raining," commented one of the barflies.

"Well, why does it always have to rain on me?" S. C. fired back. No one even tried to offer an explanation.

I was complaining the other day that whenever we go out of town, we have to find someone to take care of our daughter Antonia and our dogs, Blackjack and Goldie. George Irvine popped up and offered, "Just tie the kid to the dog and sooner or later one of them will get tired."

Dave Harmon is one of the funniest guys I know and he always comes up with good ones. He sent me a string of doctor jokes in a recent package. He says his doctor is so slow, he doesn't have magazines in his waiting room. He has novels! He says the doctor called him the other day and said, "Dave, the rabbit died."

"Quick," gasped Dave. "Is this the doctor or the garage?"

Dave says the doctor told his wife, "Frankly, I don't like the way your husband looks at all."

"I don't either," said Mrs. Harmon, "but he's nice to the kids."

Dave asked the doctor if the operation was really necessary and his doctor huffed, "Well, I guess so! I still have three payments to go on my mortgage!"

Dave says he has five kids and not one of them will come when he calls. He figures they'll grow up to be doctors or waiters.

Perhaps the best one I've heard in a while came from my daughter Antonia's little pal Tyler Selden over in Nysted. He waved me down on the gravel last week and came running up to the car, completely out of breath.

"What's up, Tyler?" I asked.

"Mom and I were driving over the Loup River at Cairo," he said with a completely straight face, "and we came on an alligator crossing the road."

"An alligator, huh?" I sniffed.

"Yep, and I had Mom stop because, Mr. Welsch, I've always wanted a pair of alligator boots."

"Yeah, then what happened, Tyler?"

"I wrestled that alligator over to the side of the road, because, Mr. Welsch, I really do want a pair of alligator boots. And then I wrestled him down in the ditch, and I got him straightened out and calmed down, and then I turned him over on his back. Man, I really wanted those alligator boots."

"Well?"

"Know what we found?"

"No, what?"

"That darned alligator wasn't even wearing boots!"

Smart aleck kid. I should have known better than to stop.

HARVESTING WOOD, CORN AND FISH

45

October 6, 1990

I have been cutting and hauling wood, figuring that we're going to have a long cold winter. I went into the post office to pick up the mail after one particularly hard morning and bill-deliverer Phil asked me why I was cutting wood on such a hot day. "Well we cut ice on cold days, don't we?" I reasoned. Phil says it comfirms everything he's ever believed about me.

Next I went over to Eric's tavern and complained about how hard I was sweating. "It's been so long since Roger's worked, he probably figures his skin is leaking," Eric deadpanned to Plumber Dan.

Betty Brown from Fairmont says that her daughter wrote home that the wind was blowing so hard in her part of the country that it kept turning on the outdoor faucets.

Paul Shold says the corn crop has been pretty good out around Dunning. He says his corn is so big that he just takes the box off his wagon and goes into the field with the running gear. He puts two, three, maybe four ears on it and drives directly to the hog pen. Once there, he makes a sharp right and then a left, and the wheels shell off enough corn for the hogs for a week.

I'm always surprised how many letters I get with pretty good lies and the writer attributes the story to someone else. Tom Goldstein, for example, says this one is told by Cecil Griffith about the Missouri River. I don't suppose Tom has ever told a lie in his life.

"The origin of Catfish Island has it that the island was originally 1½ miles upstream. A native fisherman had been unable to catch a catfish that continually broke his gear. Finally he had a blacksmith fashion a large hook. He used 3-inch manila fishline, baited the hook with a 1,500-pound steer, and make his set on the lower end of the island. Next morning, the island was downstream, at its present location, the trees shaking violently. He landed his fish but had no way of weighing it. So described his disappointment by saying, 'Its eyes were only 9 feet 3 inches apart—too close together to make a good looking fish.' So he turned it loose."

I told the story up in town but most of my fishing buddies wouldn't believe it. They said any real angler would have kept that fish for bait and opined that the yarn is probably nothing more than a fib.

Reminds me a little of Dave Harmon, who says his brother-in-law is so fat that he has to go to a truck weigh station to get weighed. He once went to a dating service and the computer matched him up with Omaha.

Dave also makes an interesting observation: "Cottage cheese makes people fat. If you don't believe me, watch people in restaurants. The ones eating cottage cheese are all fat."

GOLF AND CHICKEN DINNER

46

October 20, 1990

Delmar Sielaff of Grand Island took the time and trouble to send me a Nebraska golf tee, a tee with about three a-turns in it! I don't know much about golf, so I'll accept his explanation: "Anyone who has ever tried to play golf in this windblown state will immediately understand its purpose and how to aim it." I'll take your word for it, Delmar.

The proprietor of the Village View Farm at Bruning (he didn't give his name—bashful, I guess) was kind enough to send me a three-piece chicken dinner—three kernels of corn! And our biddy hen, Momma, sure did enjoy it, too.

Randall Gartner of Unadilla says it was so dry in Otoe County this past summer and the grasshoppers so big that one day when it rained 0.05 of an inch at his place, he came out to find a grasshopper drinking out of the rain gauge.

And Todd Carter of Palmyra says that he recently heard on the radio, a wind advisory for area lakes and toilets.

Gene Dondlinger of Shickley writes, "Farming was both good and bad around here this year. We had rain but also had a bad wind that broke over a lot of corn. The bugs were bad, too. I was getting ready to retire one night when I heard this low roar. It was a calm moonlit night and when I looked out the window I saw a large white cloud over my cornfield, going around in a big slow circle. I went outside for a closer look and it turned out to be corn borer moths circling around in a holding pattern, waiting their turn to land because there weren't enough standing stalks to accommodate the traffic."

Mike Hogan of Arvada, Colorado, says he was recently back

on the old stomping grounds and Rog Hogan, whom Mike describes as "the sage and cynic of Heartwell," was reminding him about poor old Shorty, who once tried to commit suicide by shooting himself in the head. Lucky for him, though, he was so short he missed and shot over his head.

Mike tells me to send the book award to Rog because "he would buy all of your books except he is so darn tight that he can't bring himself to pay money for something that isn't useful." Now, that really hurts my feelings. My pal Lunchbox over in Beolus says he thinks my latest book, *It's Not The End of the Earth But You Can See It From Here,* is his favorite of all my productions. Seems it is exactly thick enough to prop up the loose end of the seat in his pickup truck. ". . . Isn't useful," indeed!

Three-piece chicken dinner

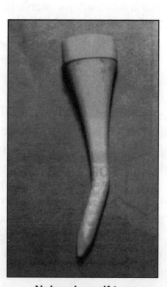

Nebraska golf tee

DRY WIT AT CLEANERS

47

November 3, 1990

I know it's not the season for "hot" stories, but then again, maybe it is. Maybe it would be yet another public service of the Liar's Corner to tell hot stories during the winter and cold stories during the summer, to smooth off some of the rougher edges of Nebraska weather. I'll think about it. Tell me what you think.

Anyway, a few columns ago I made some remarks about the liars up around O'Neill and of course right away I got letters from all sorts of Irishmen saying that it's us Germans who are the champeens in the fibbing categories. Well, by way of evidence, I submit the following letter I got from Gene Myers, who lives— you guessed it—in O'Neill:

"Dear Roger: Following is a true event that I believe you should hear. It seems to be the general conception that the farmer is the only one who is affected by the hot, dry weather. Not so! And I'd like to point out that dry-cleaners can be drought victims, also. One day this past summer, the heat and dry conditions got to the very peak, the crescendo, the all-time disaster level. It was so hot and dry that the wet steam in my dry-cleaning plant changed to dry steam. As the day progressed and the humidity dropped even further, it twisted the shafts in the humidity indicators and the little hands fell off onto the floor. The dew point disappeared and the day got even hotter and drier. The cactus plants in my office wilted and shriveled and we thought it was about as bad as it could get, but the steam got even drier, turing first to steam powder, then to dust, then to rusty dust.

"We were choking on dusty steam and brushing it from our eyes and noses. I knew we were in trouble, for if you have ever tried to press a dry pants or dress with steam so dry that it's just dust and rust puffing from your press, you know you can't flatten the skirt or poof the bust if all you've got is rusty dust.

"It was hot in that plant. The temperature was high. The cleaning was dry. The customers were dry. Even the humor was dry. I rushed to the spotting board and tried to steam out stains with the spotting gun but instead of steam, dust shot out of the gun. So instead of removing the spots with wet steam, I was sand-blasting them out with dry steam powder and making marks on the clothes as I blasted. I fooled around, making marks for a while, and then wrote some words and played a few games of cat and mouse. Then I tried blasting the company name on some larger garments and the seats of trousers. I figured, 'How many chances do I get at free advertising like this?' So I just capitalized on a bad situation and turned it into a good deal."

You know, Gene, I've seen some of those pants around town here, although for the life of me I've never understood why someone would want their name on the seat of someone else's pants. You've helped me understand the situation a little better—I think—because I've always wondered why they call it "dry cleaning."

PARANOID ABOUT A NOYD

48 *November 17, 1990*

Now, come on. I just don't know about this one. I got a letter from Perry Noyd up in Stromsburg. Perry Noyd? How can I believe anything from someone who calls himself Perry Noyd?

Anyway, Perry says that not far from Stromsburg there were two Swede brothers—are there Swedes around Stromsburg?—who couldn't get their Fordson tractor started. So they called a mechanic, who came out to their farm. He found out that the brothers had cranked that tractor so long that by the time he got there, it was overheated.

Well, I'll send a book to "Perry Noyd," but I bet I get it back labeled "Addressee Unknown." Anyone taking that bet?

Gerald Bodfield is from just down the road from Primrose Farm, over at Central City. He says he had a tough time after he got his corn in this past spring because he just couldn't get his herbicide situation straightened out. He couldn't remember whether he planted beans on the corn ground or corn on the bean ground.

But, thank goodness, he did work out a nifty system for remembering the license number on his pickup truck, a problem I have always had myself. So, I very much appreciate Gerald's scheme. He says he finally got a number he can remember; he just multiplies the first two and then subtracts that total from the third, which gives him the fourth.

That Gerald must have a lot of time to think up labor-saving devices like that. He says that when he goes out to repair fence, he just turns his cows into the pasture and they lead him to the bad spots in the fence.

I'm always uneasy when someone writes to me about his wife. Are you sure you want me to put such things in print? Gerald says he took his wife to a party not too long ago and she tried to can-can but she couldn't-couldn't. Mrs. Bodfield, that was your husband's idea, not mine.

Dave Harmon tells the one about the time his wife and he went to the dentist. "Listen," the little lady told the dentist, "I want to have a tooth removed and I want it extracted immediately. I don't care about pain or anything. Just pull it right out because we have to leave town right away. So no novocain or anything like that. Just pull out the tooth."

The dentist looked at her with admiration and said, "I have never met a person like you in all my practice. You are really a courageous woman. Which tooth is it?"

She turned and looked at Dave and said, "Show him your tooth."

Well, as Dave says, "If medical practice has made so much progress the last 30 years, how come I felt so much better 30 years ago?!"

A WORLD-RENOWNED EVENT

49

December 1, 1990

This is the one and only column of the year that is printed not only as "Roger, Over and Out" and "Liar's Corner" but which goes out over the AP news wire and appears in newspapers around the world. (No kidding. Last year I got several calls from Europe and Australia about the piece, and it was even covered in the *National Enquirer!*)

Yes, it's the annual report from the National Liars Hall of Fame:

One of the nation's most respected institutions, The National Liars Hall of Fame, held its annual awards banquet at the Dannebrog Convention Center, October 31. Official estimates of attendance ranged from four to five thousand.

Hall of Fame founder and board chairman, Roger Welsch, admitted, "It was probably closer to four. What with Saddam Hussein, Read My Lips, and congressional budget struggles, those of us who work to make folks laugh can't hold a candle to those who do it by accident."

The Hall of Fame's 1990 First Place Pinocchio Award went to Jim Taylor of Houston, Texas, who claimed that at the previous year's ceremony he ate three slabs of Liars Hall of Fame Baloney and it tripled his sex life. Taylor said, "Before I ate that sausage I used to think about sex once a week, but now I think about it three or four times a week."

Second prize went to Steve Harris at Jack's Bean Company in Grant, who said he had to fire an employee because a customer almost died of the hiccups when the worker packed a bag of beans upside down.

Moira Ferguson of Lincoln rounded out the awards with her

story that her doctor had given her only a month to live, but when he found out she didn't have the money to pay his bill, he gave her three more months.

Dishonorable mention went to Eric Nielsen, curator of the Hall of Fame. (Welsch explained that employees of the Hall are usually not eligible for Pinocchios but "Nielsen does such a bad job of curating that he just as well not be working here at all.") Nielsen reaped his prize for a comment when a Dannebrog local got the first job he had had in years: "Fred was so surprised when he started to sweat that at first he was afraid his skin was leaking."

A moment of silence was observed for the Unknown Liar, a man who reportedly introduced his wife at a banquet earlier this year with the words, "This is my wife. She was once a Miss America candidate. Of course, there were fewer Americans then."

The 1990 inductee to the National Liars Hall of Fame was a collective award to the nation's weathermen and women, "who are one of the elite groups of Americans who actually make a living telling lies." The award proved to be highly controversial however, because as many attendees later complained, "there weren't any weather tall tales this year because there wasn't hardly any weather."

WHERE TALL CORN STORIES GROW

50

January 5, 1991

Ken Niedan, president of Hershey State Bank, dropped me a line, and to my surprise it wasn't about my note being due. Ken reports that folks in Hershey are getting ready to celebrate that handsome town's centennial in 1992 and during research on the history of the town, Ken ran across some interesting newspaper reports from 1912, back when folks told nothing but the truth.

On August 22, the following curious item appeared on the front page of the *Hershey Times:*

"The news comes from up the Birdwood Creek that one of Wm. Matthewson's girls had climbed a cornstalk to see how the corn was getting along and the stalk is growing faster than she can climb down. She is out of sight. Three men have undertaken to cut down the stalk with axes and save the girl from starvation but it grows so fast that they can't hack twice in the same place. The girl is living on nothing but raw corn and has already thrown down four bushels of cobs."

Well, I would have settled for the piece of sad news, I suppose, but two weeks later, right below the ad for W. W. Young's buggies, wagons and harness, there was a follow-up to the evocative bulletin. The editor wrote:

"We would be only to [sic] glad to be able to chronicle the cornstalk girl's safe return to mother earth but as yet we cannot do so. The top of the pile of cobs she has thrown down is now out of sight and our only hope is that at the first frost the stalk will subside its prodigious growth and let the poor child descend upon the cobs.

"Still this case is not so extraordinary when you consider the wonderful productiveness of our soil out here. Why, they have to mow the grass of the sod house floors every day to find the babies.

"One family near here has twin babies with only one cradle, and the kid that has to sleep on the floor grows twice as fast as the other. Where the soil is richest a man dares not stand on one foot any length of time lest that leg become longer and bothers his walking."

He then cited similar problems published in the *Brady Vindicator:*

". . . The same week a farmer over near Curtis brought four stalks of corn to the office. His excuse was that he was afraid he could not get them into his wagon in another week.

"At a farmer's street-corner meeting in Brady last Saturday, it was unanimously adopted that in case of a boxcar shortage this fall, to ship their corn in the ear, piling it up lengthwise on flat cars."

Speaking of telling the truth in the old days, James Walker is superintendent of schools over in Stapleton, so we know we can trust anything he says, and he says that in the winter of 1935 it got so cold his father sold milk by the foot.

Finally, Dan "Flat-Out" Selden, our plumber, has been working as a roofer lately. I'm not sure I understand the connection but maybe a leak is a leak is a leak. Anyway, he says he's been working on a roof that is so steep, he has been bending nails over so that they go in straight. He says that that roof is so high, they can't get the air pressure to go far enough up the hose to drive staples into the shingles, and he is wearing an aircraft warning beacon on his shingling cap. He also claims that a couple of times when he was up on that roof, he saw eagles circling around below him, but then he lies, so I don't know what to believe.

SOME WELL-AIMED TALES

51

Nothing sweetens up the Liar's Corner more than a note from ol' Ray Harpham, Champeen Liar, down in Blue Hill. He claims that it was the cold winter of 1936 that that hill was first blue, but anyway, Ray writes:

"I suppose you wonder what became of me and tonight I am feeling sad so I will explain it to you. I hate to tell you, but Cross-Eyed Pete is gone. I think I told you about him. He is the fellow back at Holstein that was so cross-eyed when he cried, the tears ran down his back. He was always blue because he couldn't go hunting with the rest of us bull shooters, and I came up with an idea maybe we could help him.

"We did some experimenting and ran the results through that new computer we got for selling subscriptions to the *Nebraska Farmer.* It figured out how we could bend his shotgun barrel to compensate for the cross-eyes. The result was all we could hope for—ducks, doves, pheasants, all were as good as dead when he pulled the trigger.

"He was overjoyed until deer hunting season came around and he was unhappy again because he wanted to shoot a deer but he didn't have a 'compensated' rifle. So we went back to our data and came up with a curve for his rifle barrel. It was a good, high-power gun, and we did a good job on it.

"He went deer hunting as soon as the season opened up and spotted a big buck with a fine set of antlers. He aimed carefully and fired but the computer had erred slightly, so Pete missed the buck. The sad part of it was that he shot himself in the end."

Longtime readers of the Liar's Corner will remember that Ray once won the annual contest with the simplest and prettiest lie of all: "I once met an honest fisherman." He is also the one who told me about the time it was so cold in Holstein that folks were going to church just to hear about hell.

Ray is perhaps most famous for his inventing skill. I am still waiting for one of his famous iron-seated shovels.

A kind lady from over in Hartington writes to me that she never had the opportunity of an advanced education, so she has trouble sorting out the difference between words like *lay, lye,* and *lie.*

This lady, who prefers to remain anonymous—probably because she doesn't want people bothering her to write a new dictionary—says she does know one thing for sure: "If a hen sits on a nest and cackles, she's laying, but if a hen sits on the nest and clucks, she's lying."

And when that rooster crows, he's . . .

Speaking of chickens, Jean Sorenson of Marquette says she sells eggs over at her place and has a sign out by the road that says, "Eggs for sale." "The Coyotes are so bad here, I have to tie that sign down so they don't carry it away."

Now, I don't like to contradict folks good enough to write in, but that's really dumb, Jean. What you need to do is put another sign out there, right beside the egg sign, that says, "Pit-bull–greyhound-cross puppies for sale."

A STORY THAT MUSHROOMED

52

February 2, 1991

Merle Sherman from Ithaca says he has written twice before and hopes this time is the charm. (Maybe I should remind you all that I can't use every story I get—often because in the previous four years I have used the story already—and as a matter of fact, I can't even *answer* every letter.

But I do read them. I save some of them as long as a year before I can use them, and I try to get prizes out within a month of using the stories. If I ever do use your story and you don't get a book, be sure to drop me a line and remind Lovely Linda to nudge me with the cattle prod sometime in the near future.)

Anyway, Merle tells a kind of sad story, one that sounds a lot like something I might get myself into. Merle says that folks in his parts used to get together and have get-togethers, if you know what I mean. The kids would run around the yard, the gents would lie and spit, and the women would try to out-do each other in the cooking category.

Well, there was this one gathering—Merle names names, but I think I'll avoid libel problems by skipping all that—at the Joneses, and Mrs. Jones decided she was really going to put on the dog, which, as it turns out, was closer to accurate than she thought.

"She had heard about steak smothered in mushrooms and that sounded to her to be just the treat to have. The next morning she drove to town to get some mushrooms. The grocery store had some but they were in a can and were even more expensive than the rest of the meal. So she talked with Boom John (a name he earned with a gun) and he told her that what she should do is go down to the creek bottoms and pick her own mushrooms.

"Well, Mrs. Jones had heard about folks getting the wrong

kind of mushrooms, and getting sick and dying, but Boom John said he didn't take much stock in that kind of talk. 'Muskrooms is muskrooms,' he said, giving her not a lot of confidence but enough to go on down to the creek bottoms, anyway.

"She picked a mess of nice-looking mushrooms, took them home, washed them up real good, and sliced them, still a little uneasy about her amateur standing in this mushroom identification process. She cooked them and dribbled some bacon grease drippings on them and took them out to old Spot, the dog. Spot gobbled them up. Mrs. Jones watched them for a little while, but old Spot seemed just fine. In a few minutes he was back chasing squirrels and rabbits. An that was proof enough for Mrs. Jones. She cooked up the rest of the mushrooms and called the guests into supper.

"Everybody tore into the steak and mushrooms and Mrs. Jones got rave reviews, so she thought things were going along just fine, then the hired girl came in and whispered in Mrs. Jones' ear that she really hated to bother her now, but good ol' Spot was out in the yard, dying.

"You can imagine what went through Mrs. Jones' mind. She sneaked into the kitchen and called Doc Wilson, told him about the mushrooms, and Spot dying and all, and asked him what course of action he would recommend in a situation like this. He told her not to get excited, that he would be out there just as soon as he could. Meanwhile he was sending the rescue squad out with a stomach pump.

"In a few minutes the rescue squad came up with the siren screaming, sliding into the yard, throwing gravel against the side of the house, Doc Wilson right behind them. He rushed into the house with the EMTs and explained to Mrs. Jones' guests what she had told him. They set to the task, one guest at a time, and by the time they got to the last one, they were getting to be a pretty pale, peaked-looking bunch.

"About that time they got to the last sorry guest, the hired girl came crying into the house and howled at the top of her voice, 'Mrs. Jones, the really sad part is that that damned fool who ran over Spot never even stopped to see if he had killed him or not!' "

Pass the mushrooms!

WHEN THE LOAD IS TOO HEAVY

53

Art Thomsen of Alliance wrote me about his Danish grandfather, Peter Thomsen, who homesteaded near Wayside: "One day while hauling lumber from Wayside with a team of horses and a wagon, he attempted to negotiate a steep hill with a heavy load. The horses were doing their best, but to no avail. They simply couldn't pull the load over the hill.

"My grandfather looked back, and there was a little sparrow sitting on the load of lumber. Grandfather walked to the back of the load, scaring the sparrow away. Once again he whipped up the team of horses, and they immediately topped the hill."

Thirty years ago I was collecting Danish stories around Blair and someone told me a similar story about the Dane who was loading brick on the wagon and looked at his poor, weary horses. "Well, if you can pull that brick," he said, "I guess you can pull this one," and he put another brick on the wagon. And if you can pull that one, you can pull this one," and so on until the wagon was loaded with bricks, which the horses couldn't budge.

"Shoot," the old Dane muttered. "If you can't pull this brick," he said, removing a brick from the wagon, "then I guess you probably can't pull this one." And so on, until the wagon was once again empty.

Dorothy Eickhoff of Wood River says her son-in-law, Harold Plejdrup of Cairo, has such rough hands he used them to sand lumber. My wife Lovely Linda has occasionally suggested that I could do the same thing with my chin. Or my disposition.

Charles Dindlinger of Shickley wrote to me about a fellow who was burning his cornstubble, which burned quickly, and began to pose a threat to a neighbor's buildings. Seems the fire department arrived and was frantically trying to put out the fire at one end of the field while the eager farmer was doing his darnedest at the other end to get the fire burning all the way to the end of the field!

Iver Nore, over in Albion, sends a story that is one of the scariest I have heard in a long time. Sounds like the kind of stuff soap operas are made of:

"My cousin brought her husband from Minnesota to Nebraska to visit her brother. He forgot his hearing aid at home and so asked his brother-in-law, who was also hard of hearing, if he had a spare. He said he did but it needed to be cleaned because it was plugged up. After cleaning it, the visitor popped it into his ear.

"Two days later he appeared weary and conceded that he wasn't sleeping well. Seems that after unplugging the hearing aid, all the backed up conversation was released every time he dozed off, all of his sister-in-law's sweet nothings and heavy breathing kept waking him up."

Sounds like the time I loaned my glasses to Eric up at the tavern and he couldn't get anything done because through my glasses Lovely Linda looked like something out of the *Sports Illustrated* swimsuit edition. (That should keep me out of trouble with Lovely Linda for a while, don't you think?)

IN-LAWS AND LAWS OF GRAVITY

54

March 2, 1991

If any of you watch my pieces "Postcard from Nebraska" on CBS' "Sunday Morning" with Charles Kuralt, then you may recall a Christmas pageant I showed on December 23, taped at Saunders County District 74 School near Weston.

Well, the charming, lovable teacher in that school is my aunt-in-law, Helen Horacek. Her husband is Don Horacek, famed musician who has played bass with Math Slatky's wonderful band and one of my favorite in-laws from a bunch of super in-laws.

Anyway, Don has told me some of my favorite stories, and I have always considered him a champeen liar, but now he steps forth with photographs to document his last claim. He submits for your perusal this photograph showing icicles *pointing up* at the District 74 School. He says he has no idea how they came to this unusual orientation—whether the cold simply knocked out gravity for a day, or the wind was blowing straight up, or, as Don says, his exalted presence caused the icicles to stand at attention. Frankly, I think he stood on his head and took a picture of the school upside down.

Or something like that.

Paul Gibson from Canon City, Colorado (you know my reluctance to accept lies from outlying states, so to speak, but in this case . . .) tells a story that may be closer to the truth than he thinks.

He says, "In pioneer Custer County, they dammed a small valley and when it rained, that provided water for the people and the stock. When the people drank, they clenched their teeth and what went through when they drank, they swallowed, and what stopped outside their teeth, they spit away."

You know, Paul, a lot of pioneers hauled or collected water in open top barrels that sat outside the front door of the soddie. When they went out to get a drink, there was a system to it all: They rapped two or three times against the side of the barrel with the ladel, waited a second for the mosquito wigglers to go down and then quickly scooped up the cleared water from the top before the wigglers again rose.

Paul also tells about the time some locals were discussing crops at Stapleton—or maybe it was Tryon—and one braggart said he had harvested a peck of spuds from under a single vine. Jed Heldenbrand—"a notorious scoundrel," Paul says, but he says it in such a way that it sounds like a compliment—topped the day when he said that he had pulled up one of his spindly sidehill vines to see how the crop was coming and before he could stop up the hole, nearly ten bushels of 'taters' ran out.

Icicles on the District 47 school near Weston point upward, defying the laws of gravity.